MONSTROUS TALES – VOLUME 5
More long reads for late nights

Edited by Dorothy Davies

MONSTROUS TALES – VOLUME 5
More long reads for late nights

GRAVESTONE PRESS

TABLE OF CONTENTS

Sin-Eater (Damir Salkovic)

There was something about the rattle of the prison gate sliding shut that evoked finality, even if you knew you were only visiting. Some atavistic sense screamed in alarm, sent panic signals from your very marrow, urging you to get out.

Past the gate, the forbidding stone edifice of the main prison wing shrank the yard to the size of a postage stamp. Lonnie Chalmers steered the Chevrolet sedan into the visitors' parking lot, the high walls pressed closer, cutting out the powder-blue sky and the panoramic cityscape. Less than a stone's throw away, Lonnie reminded himself, gulls cried and wheeled over the bay, traffic bumped and crowded along the Coastal Highway, machinery roared and hammered down in the shipyard. But once you set foot inside Crescent Dune State Prison, the outside world ceased to exist. Only thick stone and iron bars remained, steeped in misery and suffering, a miasma of rage and hopelessness that hung over the prison like a suffocating fog.

The lot was crammed with cars. Lonnie had to drive around it twice to find a spot. He nosed the Chevy in with exaggerated care. The car was a loaner from Dick Granville, who'd sworn bloody vengeance if he found so much as a scratch on its glossy body. *Bad enough we're sending a goddam greenhorn to cover the scoop*, he'd complained to anyone within earshot, *he's doing it in my ride, too.*

Lonnie killed the ignition, sat in silence marred only by the ticking of the cooling engine. He took several deep breaths, trying to control the anxiety that crawled up his chest like a cold tide. The parking lot was full, so the viewing room would be full too, the city's top reporters jostling for the front of the pack. As a cub reporter for the San Diego Chronicle, Lonnie didn't belong among them, had no experience covering stories this big. His beat, if he could be said to have one, extended to fender-benders and council zoning decisions and melodramatic human-interest pieces. But Granville was in Washington D.C., attending a press conference on the Japanese oil embargo, Beckett was stuck in Benicia covering the munition workers' strike, and Sargisian had begged off sick, most likely with the bottle flu. That left Bob Rafferty, the Chronicle's Chief Editor, with precious few options. He'd summoned Lonnie to his office, briefly explained the assignment, and sent him out the door with a growled *don't cock this up*. As far as parting words of wisdom went, Lonnie had been on the receiving end of worse.

There was no time for contemplation. The show was underway, with or without him.

He locked the car, crossed the prison yard and went up two flights of concrete steps, presenting his credentials to a guard who had a cruel brick-colored face. The noise was enough to guide him, droning mutter, high, nervous laughter and the scrape of chair legs on a cement floor.' Another dour-faced prison screw ushered him into a shadowy chamber filled with seated people, most of them middle-aged men in cheap suits. Lonnie murmured a few greetings, nodded a few more and was roundly ignored. The front row was taken up by who he assumed were the families of the victims, elderly men and women holding hands, bodies twisted with grief, tearful faces blurry reflections in the ceiling-to-floor window that formed the room's far wall.

The space on the other side of the glass didn't look like much: a concrete box eight or nine feet across, painted in institutional pastels. Bright overhead lights burned above a heavy chair in the center of the room, slatted in the back, adorned with wrist and ankle clamps, a metal cap perched above it. Lonnie felt a sick queasiness in the pit of his stomach. When the time came, a man would be brought to sit in that chair and would never get up again.

The reporters around Lonnie shuffled and coughed and conversed in low voices. The acoustics picked up their whispers, fanned them around the gallery like flames. Several of the women in the front row were sobbing with quiet desperation, their sobs somehow all the more painful for their effort not to be heard.

One of the reporters next to Lonnie grunted out of his seat and peered over the bowed heads. "That's the families," he said to his neighbor, a heavyset man with a bulbous drinker's nose. "All four of them. Plus the Kersch girl's father."

"That was the last one?"

"Last one they found," the first man said in an ominous tone. "Can't imagine what that feels like. I got two kids of my own."

"I hope something goes wrong," said a thin type with a pencil mustache, tapping his notepad on his knee. His voice carried around the gallery like a shout. "I hope they have to fry the sonofabitch three

9

times over. If anyone deserves it, it's him, the goddamned animal."

Lonnie suddenly felt trapped in this ugly, stifling room with its competing stenches of hatred and pain, filled with the shadow of impending death. He stood up and put his hat on his chair to save his seat. Walked out of the gallery and down a long, straight corridor, trying to find a secluded spot. A smoke would help him rein in his runaway thoughts; there was still plenty of time until the main event took place. Yet the simple fact of being here was unsettling: roaming these tunnels, imagining the prisoners inside their cells, wailing, complaining, threatening, praying. Their cries soaking into the thick masonry. What a place.

He reached the end of his cigarette and the hallway almost simultaneously and was steeling himself for the return when an elevator door clattered and a uniformed guard appeared, seemingly from nowhere, to open the door. A shadow slipped out of the box, or what looked like a shadow: thin and angular, moving as if its feet never touched the ground. Of course it wasn't a shadow, but a man in a dark three-piece suit, an equally dark hat slung low over his brow. There wasn't much light in the passage, but his eyes were shaded by glasses that hid most of his sharp face.

Not a word was exchanged. The guard pivoted on his foot to open another door, this one set in an alcove, dark green and made of thick metal. Lonnie saw the man in the suit disappear through it, heard what sounded like a key in a lock, turning massive bolts. The guard picked at his teeth, leaned against the wall and sighed.

10

Moved by some urge he couldn't quite understand, Lonnie flattened himself behind a protrusion in the wall, his heart beating fast. He thought that way lay Death Row. The man in black was probably a visitor for the prisoner – a priest, or a doctor about to oversee the execution. Yet something kept him rooted to the spot: a nose for the story, he would later try to convince himself, or just one of those once-in-a-lifetime flashes of inspiration, the kind that struck like lightning from a clear sky.

If only the guard would step away for a moment.

No sooner had he thought it the uniformed man frowned, patted his bulging belly, cast a quick glance at the door and exited stage left. Lonnie waited until he heard another door close on the guard's footsteps, then went to the end of the hallway, moving as quickly as he could without making noise.

A panel in the green door showed an antechamber where another guard sat behind a desk, reading the funnies and looking bored. On the far wall was another, almost identical door. Lonnie pressed his face to the glass, praying for the guard's attention to remain on the paper. The double reflection made it hard to be certain, but he could see the cadaverous man sitting at a table, perfectly still. Someone was sitting across from him. Lonnie squinted into the gloom. Surely it couldn't be-

Then the other man leaned forward, a faint smile on his face. Lonnie felt his morning coffee and donut rush up form the back of his throat. It was Carl Bierhof, the La Jolla Strangler. The man who,

11

if Lonnie's watch was right, had less than forty-five minutes of life left.

Lonnie forgot all about the reporters in the visitor room, all about the other guard, who was probably already on his way back, who would be here any minute. Even the big scoop seemed inconsequential now. Although he couldn't hear any of it, the two men were engaged in conversation: Bierhof rocking in his chair, evidently pleased, talking, the thin man listening, nodding, adding a word here and there. The inside guard was bent over the page, studying the cartoons with rapt attention, his face blank, almost imbecilic.

Not for the first time in his twenty-three years, Lonnie Chambers felt the stomach-hollowing sensation of being in the wrong place and knowing it. But this time it was different. Something inexplicable was happening in the room, something his subconscious mind recognized and recoiled from. But he couldn't look away, no more than he could kick the prison walls to rubble, or tear the iron bars with his hands.

Vision shrank to a pinpoint. Time stretched into a thin, infinite line. If Lonnie tried, if he really put his mind to it, he could invent an exchange between the prisoner and the strange visitor, imagine a dialogue. Their voices buzzed in his skull like a bad radio broadcast.

Do you remember what brought you here?

Why wouldn't I remember? The killer laughed softly. *They said I was competent at the trial. Can't argue with that. I killed five before they caught up with me. I wish I could've killed more. Drowned this city in blood.*

12

Good. The man in black nodded, looking satisfied. *I would like you to tell me all about it. Mind, we don't have much time.*

All about it?

Spare no detail. Begin at the beginning. How did you find the first one? What told you she was the one?

She was just a girl. Bierhof seemed mildly puzzled by the question. *She was just there. Around the neighborhood. Once I got her alone, I'd know what to do. I was sure of that.*

Even though the conversation was only taking place in his head, Lonnie was appalled by the man's indifference. Carl Bierhof had strangled five young women from the middle-class neighborhoods abutting La Jolla, each time arranging the body in a lifelike pose for the family to find. Just thinking about it was enough to make Lonnie's skin crawl.

Yet instead of revolting, his mind dredged up every gory detail from the papers and the news, spewed it out in Carl Bierhof's reasonable, entirely imagined voice. With each atrocity, with each new horror, the man in black seemed to change. His face shone greasily, his eyes burned brighter, his grin wider, revealing more and more teeth. Even his body was distending, bulging in odd places, until Lonnie was no longer sure he was looking at a human being at all, but a hole in his vision, a blind spot in the approximate shape of a man.

I'm dreaming, he thought. *I'm dreaming and I'll wake up soon.*

Then it was over. The man in black pushed himself from the table, looking satisfied, like he'd

13

just had a great meal. The killer, on the other hand, seemed dazed, as if unsure where he was.

You did well, the visitor said, or rather Lonnie imagined him saying. *You did everything right. Now your work is done.*

Bierhof didn't look convinced. *I haven't finished. There is more I could do. I know there is.*

But the man in black stepped around the table, quick as a flash and seized the prisoner's head in his hands. Startled, Lonnie stepped back from the window. Surely the guard behind the door would do something now. But the man remained glued to the paper, indifferent.

Lonnie saw the visitor bend over – no, *fold* himself over, like some species of giant, hideous insect - and bring his face close to Bierhof's. Closer and closer, until their lips were almost touching. It should have looked like a kiss, but for some reason that was the last thing that came to Lonnie's mind.

Green light flared between their almost-touching lips, left bright spots floating in Lonnie's eyes. Dazed, he stumbled away from the door, into the broad chest of the first guard, who was hurrying back to his post.

"You ain't s'posed to be here," the guard said, shoving Lonnie against the wall. He jabbed a thick finger at a DO NOT ENTER sign. "Don't they teach you hacks how to read no more?"

Pressed against the rough stone, Lonnie heard a clang, saw the green door swing open. The inside guard was escorting the man in black out of the antechamber. Past their shoulders, Lonnie caught a glimpse of the La Jolla Strangler, his head lolling over the back of his chair, his mouth hanging open.

14

Then the sharp, pallid face of the visitor filled his sight, its eyes glittering so brightly that Lonnie's stomach twisted.

"He's with the press," said the guard holding Lonnie. Fear and disgust mixed in his voice as he addressed the visitor. "He didn't see nothing."

The man in black didn't respond. For a long, terrible moment, his eyes bored into Lonnie, as if trying to memorize every detail of his features. Then he smiled, nodded and tipped his hat. Without a word, he was gone, the elevator door closing behind him, sending him into the abyss.

The guard let out a long, shuddering breath, took off his hat and dabbed at his sweaty face with a not-overly-clean handkerchief.

"Get lost," the inside guard said to Lonnie. He raised his nightstick in threat. "Forget whatever you think you saw, pal, and do it in a hurry."

Lonnie didn't need to be told twice. He beat a hasty and undignified retreat to the gallery, where he found his seat taken and his hat tossed into a corner of the room. Disturbed as he was, he barely noticed. He took refuge at the back, where he dusted off his hat and tried to work out what had just happened.

What *had* he seen? Already the memory felt faded and uncertain, like something seen from afar, never fully comprehended. At most, he felt as if a vague wrongness at the center of his being, as if a mark had been seared on his soul, the recollection of vast, unimaginable pain. Had it all been a hallucination, a daydream with open eyes? It didn't bear thinking about, yet he couldn't move on from

15

it, kept going back to the incident like a tongue to a broken tooth.

There was no time for contemplation, the show was about to start. The gallery lights dimmed, throwing the death chamber into stark focus. A low murmur passed through the crowd, broken by crying. Led by two guards, a shackled Carl Bierhof walked into the chamber, taking his last half dozen steps. Lonnie made an effort to pull himself together, to focus on the story. But the look on the condemned man's face undid him. It was an expression of deep contentment, as if its wearer had seen into the heart of a cosmic mystery and moved past this world, toward some great revelation.

***

"Hey, kid."

Lonnie raised his head and a sheaf of typed pages was thrust into his face. Bob Rafferty, the Chronicle's Chief Editor, hovered over him, chewing on the end of his cigar. "This is good, greenhorn. Gotta hand it to ya. Better than I had any right to expect it to be."

Relief and excitement flooded Lonnie in equal measures. "Thank you, Sir," he heard himself say, sounding like an imbecile.

"Good enough to run." Rafferty shifted his not-inconsiderable weight. His gaze wasn't meeting Lonnie's, but wandered somewhere past him. "We'll run it on the front page."

"All right, Mr Rafferty."

"Just one thing." The pages landed on Lonnie's desk. "That fantasy thing's gotta go. The mystery

16

visitor and all. Smut like that, you can go peddle it to *Weird Tales*. This is a serious publication. I need you to cut it out, fill in another coupla hundred words."

Lonnie felt himself go cold all over. "What fantasy stuff?"

"Exactly." A meaty hand landed on Lonnie's shoulder. "Think you can get the edits back to me by five-thirty? Don't mean to rush you, but we do have a newspaper to run around here."

A bewildered Lonnie skimmed through his article. There it was, plain as day, surrounded by the Chief Editor's red slashes. He couldn't remember writing about the man in black, but apparently he had: a sentence here, half a paragraph there. The thin, shadowy presence haunted his words like a spelling error.

Could he excise it? He supposed he could, if it meant a front page piece.

Besides, the whole thing made no sense. He had seen a priest give the prisoner last rites, and his overactive imagination had supplied the rest. That was what had happened. That was the only thing that could have happened.

Comforted by his certainty, Lonnie picked up his pencil, bent over his typewriter, and went to work.

***

Over the next couple of years, the strange occurrence faded until Lonnie could no longer

17

remember any of it. Bigger things came to occupy his mind.

Indifferent to man's petty concerns, the world rolled on, caught fire and burned. Armies swarmed over hill and plain; fertile fields furrowed with trenches and barbed wire; bombs ground to dust cities and villages; ships blazed like candles and sank into the dark embrace of the sea. Less than half a year after Carl Bierhof rode the lightning at Crescent Dune State Prison, fiery death swept down from the sky over Pearl Harbor and, within twenty-four hours the nation was caught up in the whirlwind of preparations for war.

Lonnie Chalmers, now slightly older, if not particularly wiser, found himself in Manila, filling the post of war correspondent from the Pacific Theater. Against his better judgement, he followed the Ninety-First Division and General MacArthur to Corregidor, a handful of rocks scattered in the ocean over which the rival armies squandered men and materiel aplenty in pursuit of mystical and unfathomable tactical advantages. A month or so later, starving and shell-shocked and skinny as a rail, he was in the bowels of a creaking rust-bucket crammed to the portholes with wounded GIs, sailing under cover of night, in desperate flight from the Japanese advance. Smelling the stale air of the hold filled with fear and blood and the moans of the dying. Hearing the distant *crump-crump* as invading battleships pounded the island's defenses to rubble, the infernal scream of enemy Zeros strafing the retreating convoy. Feeling the battered ship buck and groan on the midnight sea.

Lonnie, falling in and out of fitful sleep, wasn't sure exactly when disaster struck, never heard the explosion, or thought to thank his lucky stars he wasn't killed outright. All he was aware of was a tremendous impact, the ship crumpling like an empty beer can and the howl of tortured metal. Up and down traded places as darkness poured into the hold, throwing him into a wall of writhing, kicking bodies. Then he was aware of the shouts of the survivors, the rush of water in the Hadean black, the sudden certainty that the ship was sinking fast, that there would be no time for him to get up to the deck and try to save himself.

Half insane with panic, Lonnie shrieked along with the other damned, flailed in the surging water. His consciousness had shrunk to a pinprick in an endless universe of sheer terror. Somehow, he clawed his way to the exit, but could go no further: arms and feet pushed him back, the cold ocean already cascading down the metal stairs, invading the ship. Something hard and heavy clubbed him with tremendous force, stars exploding in his vision. Lonnie tumbled down the steps into the freezing, surging water.

When he gasped for breath, the icy ocean filled his lungs and throat, tunneled to the very core of him, and he knew he was going to die.

Something pale floated at an indeterminate distance from him, casting a weak radiance through the flooded hold. As it drifted closer, it became a face, one that Lonnie's oxygen-starved, dying brain recognized from before. A thin, hatchet-like face, lit from within, its lips split in a sharp-toothed grin. It could have been a final vision, a death throe, but

Lonnie knew better. He remembered the awful light shining from its features, understood the question that never passed through the water, but unfurled directly in his mind like a dark, poisonous flower.

Yes, Lonnie Chalmers said, or thought he'd said. *Yes.* Faced with extinction, his being could offer no other answer, repeated it even as the thin face leaned in, as if for a kiss, as the sick green light flared behind it, turning it into a crude mask, rough holes for eyes and nose and ever-widening mouth. Even as it erased the death and cold and his own awareness spun away on that insalubrious incandescence, spinning down a deep hole in the foundations of the universe. Yes.

No other answer existed. Lonnie Chalmers wanted to live.

Stars sparkled above him. Orange light glowed on the horizon, the herald of a new dawn.

Lonnie hauled in a deep breath, thrashed in the water. Swallowed what felt like a gallon of the ocean, spluttered, almost drowned.

He was free of the sinking ship, listening to the screams of the dying. The orange glow wasn't the rising sun. It was a wall of flame, fuel leaking from the burning wrecks of the ships and it seemed as tall as the heavens. Flaming figures writhed within it, or floated motionless on the surface, or pleaded for help. Tracer bullets stitched the night sky amid the roar of airplane engines. Past the fire, the world fell away into a lightless void.

Frozen and tired, Lonnie trod the water until the last of his strength ebbed away. Then he flipped onto his back and floated, the fire gradually dying out, the sky brightening above him. He couldn't remember escaping the flooded hold, or the exact sequence of the events that preceded it, but that didn't matter. Being alive was the only thing that did.

By the time a rescue vessel found him, sunburned, dehydrated and delirious, but alive, he had convinced himself that the man in black had been no more than a hallucination. But a hidden part of him knew the truth. Without knowing how, he had crossed a boundary, stepped across a threshold into the unknown.

***

"I remember where I read it," the girl said, brushing a platinum-blonde coil behind her ear. "In your book. You know what I'm talking about. The dream? The one the protagonist has as they're waiting to get evacuated. About the shadow-man."

Lonnie nodded slowly, reached for his martini to swallow the sudden dryness in his throat. "Right. The dream. I heard that story-"

"- from a pal in the Army." She smiled at him. Very pretty, in a pale green New Look dress that swirled about her shapely calves. Her name was Joanie, or Jody, and she'd arrived on the arm of a smarmy finance executive who had fallen victim to the punch bowl and was now snoring in a spare bedroom, oblivious to the world. "I also read your interview in the Chronicle. Former cub reporter turns bestselling author. Everyone's very proud of you, Mr Chalmers."

"Call me Lonnie, please."

They were on a sofa in Bob Rafferty's living room in the Gaslamp Quarter, the girl having cornered him on the pretext of reading his fortune. Around them, the party was in full swing, bodies crowding the narrow space between Bob's bookshelves, sloshing drinks and exchanging gossip, spilling out into the back yard. Curious glances were coming their way, not all of them drawn by the girl. Lonnie Chalmers was one of the city's hotshot reporters and favored sons, his debut novel - part autobiographical, based on his wartime experience in the Pacific - a sleeper hit throughout the nation. The advance alone would have been enough for him to take a couple of years off work, but Lonnie wasn't even thirty yet and had big plans for the future.

"My editor wanted me to take that part out," he said to the girl, who crossed her legs distractingly. "He thought it didn't really fit in with the rest of the story."

"Why would he think that?"

Lonnie took a bigger gulp of his drink than he intended to, tried to look noncommittal. His throat felt tight, the walls of the room closing in, a jolt of claustrophobia riding on the tail of an unwelcome memory of the sinking ship. For no particular reason, he scanned the flushed faces of the revelers through drifting veils of cigarette smoke. Was one of them narrower than the others, hungrier, baring sharp teeth in an improbably wide smile? "He, uh, he said it was too whimsical. A fantasy that detracts from the serious tone. A hamfisted attempt at subconscious symbolism." He was meandering now, but couldn't seem to help it, his mind refusing to stay on track.

"Really?" Jody, or Joanie, was staring at him with new attention. "I took an anthropology class in my second year of college. I just *love* books about dream symbolism. Did he tell you more?"

"I'm sorry?"

"Your friend." Something in Lonnie's face must have made the girl uneasy, because her smile wavered. Instinctively she pulled back, putting as much distance between them as the sofa allowed. "The one who had the dream."

Lonnie considered his answer. "There was more," he finally said, or shouted over the blaring of the record player. A space had been cleared in the middle of the room and couples were congregating to dance. In a few sentences, he described what he had seen at the prison, careful to leave out details, framing it as another dream. "He always wondered what it all meant. If there was some deeper meaning to it. Like fate trying to send him a message." *A warning,* he almost said, but didn't. He expected the girl to lose interest in both him and his story, but her expression shifted through several emotions, finally settling on eager interest.

"A sin-eater," she said, catching a lull in Lonnie's monologue. "Eaters of filth. I studied them as part of Gaelic folklore, but the tradition exists in other places. Men and women who would consume the sins of the dying on a piece of bread. Or would get paid to do so, at least."

Lonnie said nothing. Her words, the loud music, all seemed to reach him across a great disconnect.

23

"But the light-"

"It doesn't mean anything." She waved his question away. Her eyes sparkled in the suddenly dim room. "The sins can't be given back, or passed to someone else. It doesn't work that way."

"It doesn't?"

"Unless they're accepted willingly," the girl said, matter-of-fact. "Hey, are you okay? You don't look so swell."

Unless they're accepted willingly. The words sat in Lonnie's stomach like cold water. Like the gallons of the Pacific he'd swallowed after the sinking of his ship. It wasn't the right explanation, he knew that. There was nothing merciful or benign about the figure in black. Only sheer malevolence, wafting off it like a bad smell. But there was a kernel of truth in it, a revelation as yet ungrasped. "How does one get rid of them? The sins, I mean?"

"Would you really want to?" Jody, or Joanie, got up in one graceful movement, held out a manicured hand. "Enough about dreams, Mr Chalmers. I believe San Diego's bestselling writer owes me a dance."

***

Cliched as it may sound, the first step to finding something is to start looking for it. Once Lonnie started looking for the man in black, the enigmatic figure seemed to be everywhere.

He was a secretive fellow, the thin man: he preferred to do his work on the sly, to stick to the shadows. But by the time the rigid fifties gave way to the swinging sixties, Lonnie Chalmers was a major name in investigative journalism, his columns syndicated in the nation's most read newspapers, with ways and means and his own network of contacts on both coasts and everywhere in between. Moreover, he intended to use it.

On the surface, Lonnie lived under a charmed star. A second novel had seen the light of publication, receiving both critical acclaim and encouraging sales. One of New York's major publishers had forked out a sizable advance on a new book, a non-fictional account of his experiences as a wartime correspondent. It was the book that undid him, or rather his attempts to write it. Because the harder he tried to remember, the more his memory abandoned him, fractured into hundreds of confounding shards, replaced by the gift he'd accepted on that fateful night at sea.

Each time he sat down behind his typewriter, a pack of Newports and an ashtray at his right elbow, a fresh bottle of Scotch by his left, a hole seemed to open up in the blank page and that blankness would invade the space behind his eyes. Most times he'd just sit in his chair for hours, unable to muster out a single word. But other times the greyness parted like mist and he found himself on a wide plain, or a bleak shore, or on a long road winding into infinity. A negative-image world, as if the heavens and earth had been turned inside out. There were others in this dreadful place, figures moving around him: men and women and children, old and young, some wrapped in dirty rags, some naked and shivering, others yet clad in finery from times long gone by. All stamped by rage and violence and suffering,

25

victim and tormentor standing shoulder to shoulder. Bloodied, broken soldiers next to infants blackened with pox. Slaughtered natives, entire tribes of them, appearing and vanishing like ghosts, their eyes aglow in the blur. Troops of uniformed horsemen with ragged, gaping wounds, mounted on skeletal nags, chasing one another across the landscape, never getting closer. Slaveholder next to whipped, shackled slave; burned men with nooses around their necks walking alongside night riders and hooded klansmen. An endless procession of sorrow and loss, wandering this land of the damned forever.

Each time the vision would release him more reluctantly, piece by painful piece and he knew that there would come a day when the thin man's gift erased the last vestige of Lonnie Chalmers, there would be nothing left. It was as if the investment of centuries of sin, of all that accumulated petty evil and misery, was about to bear some unthinkable dividend, a rotten and stinking fruit growing from a bad seed sown in the loam of human spirit.

Joanie had told him as much in those last vitriol-filled months before the divorce. *I don't know who you are anymore. Not the man I married.* But Joanie was wrong. He'd ceased being himself long before he'd met her. Lonnie had something that belonged to the man in black and his existence, his very soul, depended on giving it back. So he spent long days and sleepless nights perusing newspaper archives and the dusty back shelves of libraries, determined to learn more about his nemesis.

Because every living thing had to feed to survive. It was just a matter of working out the pattern.

He found the narrow face hovering in the background of a grainy photograph commemorating a lynching in Mississippi; soaking up the pain and anguish in an all-black church in Chicago after a deadly race riot, apparently unnoticed by the mourners; peering behind a row of smiling men posed proudly around a charred corpse, his hand on the shoulder of a grinning, strapping blond youth. Now, years later, a great upheaval was underway: the nation's oldest and vilest sins were being unburied, setting loose a fresh wave of atrocities. The creature - Lonnie no longer thought of the thin man as human - had gone into a feeding frenzy. Throwing caution to the wind, it followed the trail of activist marches and the bloody blowback they evoked, gorging itself on the agony and rage and evil left in their wake. For all its abilities, supernatural or otherwise, it could no more help itself than a shark in chummed water.

Everywhere it went, Lonnie Chalmers would follow, reporting from the heart of the bloodshed, his articles reaching millions of his bewildered countrymen over their morning coffee and toast.

The Chronicle grew its readership, expanded its circulation and was bought out by a Los Angeles media syndicate. Bob Rafferty retired after his second heart attack, was replaced by a mutton-chopped East Coast transplant barely a few years older than Lonnie, who wore his hair long and padded his speech with words like *groovy* and *outtasight*. Mutton Chops lasted all of two fiscal cycles, after which the Chief Editor's seat was filled by a bright-eyed Princeton graduate more adept at editing profit-and-loss statements than articles. A President was assassinated; mankind skimmed the black rim of space; the Summer of Love flooded the streets with flowers and song.

If Lonnie noticed any of these events, it was only in passing, or as background noise on the radio. He spent his days in trains and buses and rental cars, his nights drinking and cross-referencing newspaper articles and road maps, plotting his route. He caught a glimpse of the man in black at the far end of the crowd, or prowling the fringes of a funeral, or separated from him by a wall of red-faced, scowling policemen. Closing the distance, but always a step behind. What he would do when he caught up with the creature, how he would force it to take its gift back: these questions never crossed his mind, for he wouldn't let them. He would cross that bridge when he came to it. Pushing the thought aside, he drove himself on, consumed by his obsession.

***

A dull roar came from the front as the men on the bridge advanced. The crowd wavered, lost its shape and broke apart. Shots filled the hot, sullen air, followed by a chorus of agonized cries, the thundering of horses' hooves.

Trapped between the men and women in the back and those retreating from the front, Lonnie saw a child in a Sunday dress fall to the hot asphalt and disappear under a flurry of bodies and feet. Blows

28

rained from all sides, the gas-masked troopers swinging their nightsticks, the panicked marchers flailing as they ran for their lives. He dove into the melee, flung himself over the small shape. Picked the wailing girl up and thrust her into a pair of outstretched arms.

It was the ship all over again: bodies pushing back against him in mindless fear, the walls caving in, the certainty of impending death. He tried to shove free, but could no longer see a way out. His eyes, his nose, his entire face burned as if on fire. A stick slammed cruelly into his midsection; another missed his head by inches. A foaming horse rushed at him from the billowing tear gas like a nightmare fury, almost trampling him. Lonnie flung himself aside, landed painfully, scrambled up as quickly as he could. Before he could find his bearings, something small and fast whizzed straight at him from the smoke. Darkness crashed around him as soon as he felt the impact and he knew no more.

He woke up in a hospital ward in the middle of the night, dizzy and parched, his whole body a mass of raw pain. Ceiling fans stirred the hot, humid air. A bandage held his throbbing head intact and he was bruised all over, at least a couple of ribs broken and teeth loose in their sockets, his every breath an agony. From what he could piece together, he'd been knocked out by a tear gas canister, after which the troopers had worked him over with their nightsticks and hobnailed boots.

Groping about for the cord, he rang the bell, croaked weakly for help, but none came. His coverage of the march had won him no friends here. He was lucky to be alive, would be luckier still if no

29

proud Son of the South snuck in under the cloak of darkness to finish the job.

Gradually he became aware of eyes watching him. A slender shape, blacker than the night, crouched on the bed opposite his: the sharp outline of hat, then the pale sliver of a face, the rest of the angular body unfolding slowly beneath it, a spider crouching in the center of his web. Lonnie closed his eyes as the creature leaned over the bed's occupant and started to feed. Yet the flashes of green light seemed to find their way through his tightly shut eyelids, to sear into the very meat of his brain.

The noises stopped and he heard the clack of patent-leather shoes on the worn linoleum. Drawing nearer, each sharp tap echoing as though down an infinite corridor.

He felt a presence at his side, the fever-heat of that hatchet face bending toward his. But he refused to open his eyes. If he didn't look, if he refused to acknowledge the thing, it couldn't hurt him. The thought made no sense, but Lonnie wanted to believe it anyway.

A hideous reek filled his nostrils: wet ashes, burning flesh, bloated corpses dredged up from the bottom of the ocean, releasing the vapors of decay. Damp, cold worms wriggled in his ear. Lonnie hauled himself off the bed, screaming, crashed to the floor in an explosion of pain. His eyes sprang open.

Save for a few patients asleep in the beds, the ward was empty. An open window swung gently at the end of the aisle, letting in the orange glow of the streetlamps. A breath of breeze stirred the curtains, then they were still.

Lonnie crawled to the window, raised himself over the sill. The man in black was standing on the sidewalk, looking up at him. There was something odd about the creature's shadow: it spilled like oil across the cracked pavement, absorbing all light.

Without a sound, a black Corvette pulled up to the curb. Lonnie shook his head, blinked to clear his sight. The car seemed to waver in and out of focus, to defy all attempts his mauled brain made to fix it in reality. Here was his chance to challenge the thin man, to tear away the creature's disguise, and behold its secret face. Perhaps his life would be returned to him, or perhaps he would endure some other, much worse fate. Either way, it would be over.

But the words wouldn't cross his lips. A moment passed like a year, then another, and hesitation snatched the opportunity away. The man in black grinned, cocked his finger into a pistol, tipped his hat at Lonnie. He hopped into the car, which pulled away from the sidewalk and vanished into the night.

***

The bartender didn't like the look of the drunk at the end of the counter. Hardly five in the afternoon, the sun still strong, and the guy was already out of his skull, his eyes closed, his grizzled head weaving slightly from side to side. It gave the place a bad image, kind of like one of those kitschy retirement communities for aging alcoholics in

31

Florida, not a hip and trendy bar in the city's up-and-coming historic beach district.

"Hey." He approached cautiously, prodded the man's shoulder. "Hey, pal. You think it might be time for you to move on? Get on home, or something?"

Rheumy eyes snapped open, stared around wildly for a second, squinted against the slanting late afternoon light. "Got the time, sport?"

The bartender told him. Looking wistful, the drunk swayed himself upright, grabbed the edge of the counter. Teetered, but kept his feet.

"Guess it's about that hour," he said, plopping down a twenty. "Tide'll be in any minute now."

"Whatever you say, man." The bartender picked up the twenty, pretended to fuss with the till until the old man waved his change away. Maybe it was the tip that softened his heart, but he felt a pang of regret as he watched the other stagger out the door. The codger was a regular who drank like it was going out of style, but never made a fuss, always paid up and tipped well. A long time ago he'd been a writer, or a journalist, supposedly a big name. Now it was all he could do not to pass out under a table and piss his pants in the bargain.

Whatever the word, the bartender had already heard it. In this year of our Lord nineteen eighty-two, every decrepit boozer had a story he just couldn't wait to spill. *Forget self-actualization courses and all that Human Potential claptrap*, the bartender thought as sunlight flared on the closing door, erasing the old man from sight. *This is what it all comes down to. For all of us, if we're lucky to*

32

last that long. Slumped over the bar, looking for the truth at the bottom of the bottle.

Pleased with his astute observation, he turned to the coruscating bottles, picked up a glass and started to polish it.

***

Sun in his crinkled eyes, Lonnie Chalmers descended to the old pier, down to the remains of the boardwalk, where murky water laved the decayed pilings.

In his childhood and youth, the boardwalk had been one of the city's main attractions, packed with locals and vacationers seven days a week, with a Ferris wheel and arcades and vendor stalls selling hot dogs and cotton candy and sodas from morning to night. Now only the husks remained, boarded up and covered in posters and scrawled with graffiti, the bright paint on the still-standing walls scoured away by decades of Pacific winds, sun and rain. Past the former Palisades Theater the promenade was sectioned off by construction barriers and warning signs. A huge billboard advertised a luxury condo community with a view of the sea.

Lonnie skirted the signs, ducked under the railing and lowered himself onto the rotting timbers. His right knee creaked in protest: his left one, smashed in by a baseball bat on a hot night in Alabama in the distant past, almost refused to straighten out again. He winced, picked his way carefully to where the boards curved out to sea, then clambered onto a heap of torn-up wood, the remains of the promontory.

33

It was a calm day, the bay as smooth as glass, no more than a hint of white crests out on the open water. It smelled of salt and stone, but also of the secret places under the boards where the sun never reached, where things crawled and slithered in eternal twilight, things that belonged neither to the night nor the day. Lonnie breathed in the smell, pulled in as much of it as his wheezing lungs would allow.

When he turned round, the thin man was standing in the mouth of a huge pipe, not touched by the reddish sunlight, nor covered completely by the darkness behind him.

Lonnie had hoped to find the creature here and was afraid that he would. But it was done now. Whatever question he wanted to ask, whatever curse or accusation he wanted to fling into that thin, predatory face, had lost all meaning years ago. It was gone now, just as the rest of him was gone. He had spent his life, his health, chasing this pallid specter. There had to be a reason for it all, but he wouldn't get an answer from the thing in the pipe. For all its power, it was no closer to understanding its nature, its true role in the universe, than anyone else.

All that was left to say was, "You came back."

The thin man made no sign of having heard, or understood. Lonnie held his arms out. A meaningless gesture, but one he thought the creature understood.

"Take it back," he said. "I was wrong. I don't want it. I never did."

The creature understood. It smiled and Lonnie instantly knew everything there was to know.

34

He glanced over the promontory's railing, at the lapping waves, the rocks and concrete slabs below. Twenty-five feet, maybe thirty. If he got lucky, it could be over soon. But he didn't really believe that, couldn't bring himself to try and he sensed that the man in black knew it too.

Immense pain hollowed him out, something hard and jagged tearing free from the center of him, then was gone.

It took Lonnie a moment to realize that the void it left behind, the emptiness, was even worse.

On the other side of the bay, lights were coming on in an unfamiliar skyline. Traffic blinked down what to Lonnie would forever be the new highway, the one built right after the war. Matchbox houses and apartment buildings sprouted from the gentrified bones of factories, windows catching the sunset above Long Beach Naval Shipyard.

As much as the world had changed, it would always remain the same. There was a lot of sin out in it, unseen undercurrents running right beneath its skin. A thousand sin-eaters, a million, couldn't keep up with this rootless century, the hustle and envy and greed that pumped through its rotten, beating heart.

There would always be room for one more.

Lonnie Chalmers stepped away from the railing. clamped a cigarette between his teeth and cupped a hand around his lighter, against a sudden cold gust from the sea.

By the time he exhaled the first sinful cloud of bluish smoke, the thin man was gone but he'd left a new present in the darkness of the tunnel, a patch of black darker than the shadows. Lonnie walked in, fingered the fine fabric. A three-piece suit, shirt, tie, and shoes, all laid out neatly on an upturned paint can. Two steps beyond the clothes, a matte black hat hung from a twist of wire. It looked a bit like the hats the bad guys wore in old movies, a bit anachronistic, but there was a certain flair to it, what they called retro these days.

He held up the clothes. They felt smooth and cool to the touch, like silk. The trousers were a bit short, the waist a size or two too small. But that didn't matter. In time, it would fit him perfectly, like a second skin.

Lonnie left the clothes behind him and went back out onto the promontory. He smoked as the night ate the sea, the sky, as the glittering constellation of the city came out in full brightness, and when he was finished he lit another.

Dangerous Ground (Sandra Stephens)

On the last run of the day he saw it.

It was 55 degrees and sunny, a true bluebird day and Ken Porter was getting in a couple of runs after meeting with Cindy Maxwell, the local realtor he'd hired to sell the old family cabin. Cindy was a coiffed blonde with a shark-like smile who assured him it was a hot market, she'd sold two properties in Tahoe Pines in the past six months and saw a quick sale in the Porter cabin though it hadn't been updated in decades.

"Authenticity is in," she told him without a shred of irony. Ken didn't care. All he wanted was a quick sale and to get back to Chicago.

He was skiing The Meadows, a local hill that didn't get as much traffic as the big operations now owned by Vail. After a few runs he took Scott's chair at the far western edge of the resort, which dumped skiers onto a ridgeline - to the right, a series of fast blue groomers, to the left on the other side of the ridge the Palisades backcountry, where the sun was warming the slopes to perfect corn snow. For his first two runs, he went right; after ten years of driving the desk of a corporate lawyer, he wasn't sure he was up to the challenge of double black diamonds. The ghost of his old friends mocked him. The Palisades had always been a favorite run of his brother Thad and their friends.

It was his first trip back to the Sierra Nevadas in more than twenty years, his first time back on skis in ten. It was a weekday and he had the chair lift to himself, only a handful of skiers dotting the slopes - mostly locals and ski bums. Ken was neither, though at one time he'd been both The trip had two goals: go through Thad's stuff, one by one consigning his personal effects to sell, store, or incinerate. Then, put the cabin on the market. The sale would sever Ken's last tie to his childhood, which suited him just fine. Nothing about it had turned out well. This trip was a bad coda to a story he'd never chosen to live.

There was no body to bury or cremate to scatter ashes, even if Ken were the sentimental type, which he wasn't. Just tons of rock and ice and, under it somewhere, Thad's smashed middle-aged body. Thad, who worked ski patrol at a local hill, was killed in something the resort's lawyers tactfully termed "an avalanche control miscalculation". There was more to it, Ken knew. With Thad, there always was.

It would take heavy moving equipment to bring him down, the resort manager explained. Probably not 'til June, after the snow and ice melted.

Ken was resigned. Coming back again would be inconvenient but was not unexpected. He was glad there was no talk of pressing charges against Thad's estate, such as it was. From what Ken could gather, Thad was not assigned ("or even expected" the resort manager said carefully) to be on the mountain doing avalanche control early that morning. 'Early morning' meant the dead of night.

"We're still trying to figure out what happened," the resort manager told him. "I'm sorry for your loss, Mr. Porter. Thad was one of a kind and he knew these mountains better than anyone."

There was an ambiguity to this send-off not lost on Ken. That Thad had used explosives ("a lot of them", the resort manager emphasized) taken from the resort and blasted them in an unauthorized area was clearly a crime, but the resort was reluctant to press charges against a dead man who'd been popular.

What in the world had Thad been up to? Ken thought he knew. Just like anyone who'd known their father would think *they* knew. Though it turned out they were all wrong.

***

He was boarding the Scott chairlift for the third time a woman in a green ski patrol jacket swooshed up.

"Join?" she asked pleasantly and, though Ken would rather be alone, he nodded. It was good ski etiquette to defer to ski patrol.

"Knock yourself out," he said.

"Let's hope not," she smiled.

They chitchatted as the chair whirred forward... when Ken revealed why he was in town, she turned on the narrow bench to face him fully, her uphill ski swinging out over empty space.

"You're *Thad's* brother?" she asked. "Wow. I'm so sorry. I really mean that."

"Thanks." He stared out over the mountains, feeling her eyes on his face. He pointed a ski-gloved hand at his chest.

"Ken."

"Chelsea."

"So you knew Thad?"

39

"Everyone knows Thad. Knew Thad. God I'm so sorry," She threw him a stricken little look. "We used to hang out sometimes. He was a really sweet guy. A little... I don't know."

"Crazy?" His voice more bitter than he intended.

She tilted her head. "I was going to say, lost."

Ken smiled. "So you liked him." Trying not to sound surprised.

That head tilt again. "Everyone liked Thad. And no one knew the mountain better than him. That's what made the... accident so hard to believe, you know?"

Ken noted the hesitation. The chair lift creaked and squeaked its way upward, gliding its shadow over a snowboarder resting flat on his back on a mogul run. Why he assumed it was his back and not her back Ken wasn't sure - the baggy pants, brightly colored helmet, mirror goggles were as ubiquitous as they were anonymizing, concealing the curves of hips and breast. Still he knew it was a he. Instinct, maybe.

"They can't get the body down 'til June," he told Chelsea, even as a voice inside was saying *Jesus Christ don't tell her about that, no one wants to hear about that!* Something about the sympathy in her face unlocked his mouth.

"So on this trip it's about getting the cabin ready for sale."

They were silent as the chair hummed up into the blue.

"Well, it's a superhot market these days," Chelsea said. "Or so I'm told. Nothing the likes of

40

little old me can afford." She laughed a mirthless laugh.

"My realtor says authenticity is in," he said, mimicking the realtor's sharky white smile. Chelsea laughed, the sound pealing out over the expanse of snow lining the bowl beneath the chair.

"Idiot's delight."

"I beg your pardon?" For a confused second Ken thought she was talking about the realtor. Or himself. But Chelsea's face was solemn, unsmiling.

"Idiot's Delight is the run you have to take. Then traverse over the ridge to get to the cliff where they were doing avalanche control. It's all blocked off, though. You can't really get near it."

Where Thad was killed, she meant. Where his body lay still buried beneath tons of rock, ice and dirt.

Ken imagined Thad - not the grizzled whip thin mountain man he was when he died, but as he was in Chicago, still young and floppy-haired - curled in a fetal position, sleeping untouched beneath an avalanche of ice and rock, Sleeping Dirtbag instead of Sleeping Beauty.

"Why not?" he asked. Thad's accident had been more than three weeks ago; there'd been no new snow since then.

She frowned. "So many boulders were displaced by the blast. It's dangerous ground over there."

Then the ground was rushing up to meet their skis and they were disembarking, she with a smooth professional insouciance and he with a faint hurry and flurry that embarrassed him. She pulled her

41

goggles down, so all he could see were twin suns reflecting back at him. "Which way you headed?"

"The Pallisades," he told her. She nodded. It was the opposite direction from Thad's resting place, if being smashed into immobility could be called resting.

"I'm headed down to the lodge, gotta pick something up before the office closes," she said. "It was nice to meet you, Ken, though I'm real sorry for the reason for meeting." Her head tilted, twin suns burning in the mirrored irises of her goggles.

He was thinking what to say when she gave a little wave and went right, down a short steep hill leading to a longer, steeper run. Her skiing was graceful and effortless, the same as all ski instructors. The same as Thad. Ken too had skied that way, at one time. It was fun, but like most fun things it didn't pay the bills.

***

They grew up on the north shore of the lake, in Truckee. His mom told them the word Truckee was a local indigenous word meaning "everything is all right". She was always telling them things like that.

Thad was only six when she left town with an Argentinian ski instructor. Ken, who was twelve, remembered her better. Memory was pretty much all they had left - after her defection their father's incipient drinking problem became full blown alcoholism. He tossed all of his wife's clothes, books, toiletries and even her yarn basket trailing long dreds of color into the back of the truck. He ordered the boys into the cab.

"You boys want to roast marshmallows?" he asked with a threatening joviality that had scared Ken badly, though he tried not to show it. Thad, missing his mom and terrified of this beer-breathed monster wearing daddy's face, had cried, his little chin tucked hard against his chest. Ken buckled Thad into his seatbelt, whispering "Quiet, baby brother."

His dad drove to a place locals sometimes used for target shooting, referred to for some obscure reason as the Gallery - a large plateau of cracked concrete in the middle of a canyon, surrounded by dense forest. There, their father piled his errant wife's belongings in an untidy heap, soaked it with gasoline and set it ablaze. He handed each of his boys a sharpened stick with a marshmallow speared at the tip and they roasted them, Ken holding Thad's stick when the flames became too hot for the limited reach of his six year old arms.

Their marshmallows browned while they watched her belongings burn. The Fleetwood Mac vinyl collection. Her blue beret, the long tie dye dress that she wore in the summer. Her yellow heart-shaped sunglasses. A tangle of bras, underwear and swimming suits. Her macrame purse still full of her chapstick, packet of tissues, pens, carabiners, keys and change purse. Everything except the familiar green down jacket and red ski pants. her ski patrol uniform she'd been wearing when she left that morning, never to return.

Thad sniffled and Ken saw a flash of blue. It was the turquoise pendant she wore all the time, even skiing - a round disc of turquoise with a thin silver edge like a moon, always cool to the touch.

When he was Thad's age, Ken would reach up to finger it while she sat at the edge of his bed reading him a story. Without thinking he snatched the earring, making a little hiss when it scorched his fingers. He pocketed it with a quick glance at their dad, who was nodding off in a lawn chair, a tall can of Milwaukee's Best (the Beast, as he called it) propped in his crotch and a carbonized marshmallow on a stick drooping from his hand.

When the fire burned down, their father unzipped his fly. "Come on, boys, let's piss on her!" he cried with that same threatening joviality in his voice when he invited them to roast marshmallows. A voice that carried an implicit "or else".

"I don't have to go," Ken said.

His father handed him the Beast, now warm from the fire. Ken took a sip, hating the taste of it.

"Jesus, kid, DRINK IT!" his father yelled and Ken downed three huge gulps that made his throat burn. He burped and his father laughed with no humor. "Give a kid a goddamn beer! You'd think he'd be happy but not this one, no. Like your mother, I guess."

Ken had to help Thad navigate the escape hatch of his snow pants. He was crying again, but silently this time. He leaked a few drops from his tiny boy's penis. "Atta, Thaddy," his dad's laughter an uncomfortable howl. Thad cried harder.

The beer did its work and Ken was able to produce a short stream that satisfied his father. His father clapped him on the back and said "Atta boy, Kenninator! A chip off the old block!"

That night Ken got Thad ready for bed. Downstairs on the couch, their dad snored off the depleted bottle of Smirnoff's. He snapped off the light and closed the door, but Thad's voice stopped him.

"Kenny, do you think the fan man took Mommy?"

"Nobody took Mommy," Ken told him. "She went to visit her friend." Much later he would pinpoint this moment as the one when anger at her birthed itself in his belly.

Thad was silent.

"What's a fan man, Thadder?"

Thad sat up, his fists next to his cheeks. All at once his fingers popped open, fan-like, on either side of his face.

"He does that when he's nervous, Mom says. I think the fan man wanted her to visit him. I miss her." His voice was sleepy.

"She misses you too, Thaddy. Look here, what she left you." He held up the turquoise pendant. Thad reached for it, fingering the stone without taking it.

"Did she really?" he asked, without looking at Ken.

"I'm 100% positive she wants you to have it," Ken said.

Thad took the pendant, puddling the chain into his palm before sliding it under his pillow.

"Now go to sleep, bud, everything's going to be okay."

Thad's voice small in the dark. "All right."

***

On the last run of the day Ken saw the green flash of a ski patrol jacket near the base of Scott chair, where three trails converged at a log cabin cafe and another lift.

"Chelsea!"

She swooshed over and invited him for an apres beer at Bridgetender, a local bar. At the name he felt another one of those little jolts of familiarity he'd been having since driving up from Reno airport and through Tahoe City.

He hesitated. He hadn't planned on looking up any old friends, wasn't ready to see someone who might recognize him, talk about Thad. She seemed to read his thoughts.

"I'm meeting some friends. How about after, I bring a six pack over to your place?"

Still he hesitated. It wasn't just that she looked awfully young. Thad's decorations were... unique and Ken hadn't had time to clear even half the surfaces.

"Or not," she added, with an endearingly crooked smile.

"It's not that," he started to say.

"It's not *anything*," she laughed. "Just a beer."

"Okay," he said. "But fair warning, there aren't a whole lot of places to set a beer."

"We'll just hold them then. Or better yet, sit outside on the deck."

Behind them the lift operator announced through a bullhorn with a unicorn horn on it that the lift would close in thirty minutes.

"Done for the day?" he asked her.

"No way, I'm just swapping out skis for my snowboard for the last couple of runs!" She was already sliding away from him.. "See you at six. Or seven!"

***

He leaned back in the chair, arms wide, occasionally tilting his face to the sun, no longer overhead but no less bright. It was three thirty, enough time for another run - two if he was feeling aggressive. He wasn't, but it was nice to pretend like he might. He felt a warmth in his chest that might be the late afternoon sun... or anticipation, that long-lost friend.

The run beneath the lift was dappled in shadow; the snow in the sun would be perfect corn snow but the shadowed snow would be crunchy. A skier went scraping down the slope, skis rattling against the crusted ice of the top layer. Fifty yards upslope, in a copse of trees littered with boulders, his eye fell on it.

He still didn't see it, at first, though he was gazing right at it. Its camouflage on the snowy, shadowy slope was perfect. Then the boulder he was looking at, one among many, shifted, stretched and stood up. Ken caught his breath, a confused gladness washing through him. For a second he almost lifted his hand, shouted Thad's name. Something about the way the figure stood, its face lifted to the sun, reminded him powerfully of his brother.

47

Then the illusion snapped. Just a kid in a costume, a common sight on spring skiing days as perfect at this one.

Except there was no snowboard or skis or poles around.

Maybe someone who walked down from the top, looking for something dropped off the lift, he thought.

The chair lift passed over it and Ken leaned forward for a closer look, still thinking it was a kid in a costume - a full body latex suit that fit like a second skin. Then he saw the steam rising off it.

Gray-green eyes opened, staring directly into his own hidden behind polarized goggles. The chatoyant eyes widened, a frilled fringe of skin unfurling from its forehead, cheeks and neck. There was a sound like air leaking forcefully from a tire. A flash of white he realized were its teeth. It was hissing at him.

Then it was running upslope in an easy muscular scramble, almost but not quite on all fours. At the top, silhouetted against the ridge, it looked back up at him, the frilled fringe folding down around its bullet head.

Keeping his eyes on it, Ken slowly extracted his iPhone from his pocket. He lifted it, just as the thing turned and leaped downslope into the backcountry. His arm was fully extended and he was leaning forward against the restraining bar when his ski tips slammed into the snow berm built up on the lift exit. The chair pulled him forward out of his skis.

The bored young lift operator stopped the chair while Ken clicked sheepishly back into his skis and retrieved his poles.

"Sorry," he told him. He wanted to ask, "Did you see that?" but knew the answer without asking.

See what, the bored kid would ask in a bored voice, figuring Ken was just trying to cover for his dumb rookie mistake of falling off the lift.

And then what would he say? *A steaming boulder-skinned fan-faced lizard creature with green eyes? About this tall? Totally shredded abs?*

He checked his phone but the picture he'd managed showed only a blur disappearing over a snowy ridge - it could have been anything.

It had moved with such strength and ease and purpose. Like it knew the terrain well.

Ken's legs went rubbery at the thought of that thing coming back over the ridge. He could never outski it, he knew. Thad might, but not him.

A skier zipped past him and cut right, taking one of the fast blue runs. Ken followed. The snow was heavy and choppy. He was trying to ski fast but had become too conservative, mindful of his softening quads and hardening Achilles. His mind was screaming *It's real, it's really real, that thing was real all along.*

***

When their father finally died of cirrhosis, Ken was a senior, Thad in junior high. There was no funeral. He was cremated, the ashes interred in a cheap plastic urn. There was a small notice in the paper, after which a few people from town left gifts on the porch - casseroles, a sack of potatoes, some hand-me-down jackets and hats. A realtor stopped by and left her card stuck in a crack between the door and the jamb; Ken put it in the kitchen junk drawer.

There was no bank account, no stocks, just the cabin, which his father had paid off before the Argentine ski instructor days, before the booze and anger and resentment had their way with him. A local lawyer helped Ken navigate the process to become Thad's legal guardian. Ken was officially on the hook to keep the electricity and water on and enough food to live on, which he had been doing unofficially for the past decade anyway.

Thad pitched in working whatever jobs he could pick up: a bike shop, repairing snowboards, snowplowing, Army surplus. He worked for two years at a camera shop the next town over; there was the semester he worked as an assistant to a professor at UC Davis, mapping mycelium networks in the Sierra Nevadas, commuting - usually by hitchhiking - to the campus one day a week for five months. It seemed there was no rhyme or reason to his career path, except the minimal support needed to survive. Or so it seemed to Ken, whose plodding journey to corporate lawyer had been as steady as it was uninspired. Safety was what he was after.

***

Ken looked around the cabin at Thad's possessions - almost exclusively mementos from each job he'd held over the years - another picture was coming into focus. The night vision goggles from the army surplus store. The mountain bike with its big treaded tires and eighteen inch travel for riding fast where most people wouldn't - couldn't - dare to go. The rock climbing harnesses and shoes, the chalk. The skis for every terrain, the ice axe. The cameras and telephoto lenses.

A pile of random equipment…. or tools for the job at hand?

Before this trip he would have cracked that Thad's job was dirtbag esquire. Now he knew what the job was, had been all along.

Thad was searching for their Mom. And whatever took her. The fan man - the thing little Thad had told him about, a thing Ken had never believed in, belief that had changed in the blink of a chatoyant eye.

***

Thad only visited him in Chicago once. He acted antsy and bored, looking at everything Ken had to show him with a lack of engagement that made Ken want to clock him one. Still it was mostly a good trip. He took Thad to Smith and Wollensky's for steak and Chicago Blues for music and Wrigley Field for baseball. Thad insisted on cooking trout almondine when he discovered vendors selling the whole fish at the farmer's market.

"Move up here, you can make me dinner every night," Ken joked.

Thad smiled, drank his beer from the bottle, looking around the bar lounge with its glass tables and low pouf seating.

"It's not the Bridgetender, is it?" he cracked.

But Ken persisted. "I've got two bedrooms."

Thad tipped his long neck toward Ken in acknowledgement. "Thanks, brother. But I gotta be getting back."

"It's summer." Thad's job as ski patrol wouldn't demand anything from him for months yet.

Thad drank his beer.

"Come on, man. There's nothing keeping you there." Part statement, part question.

"It's where she is."

At first Ken thought Thad was referring to a woman - a girlfriend. Then he realized.

"There's nothing left of her there, man. You know that."

Thad shrugged, avoided Ken's eyes. "Says you."

"We were *kids,* Thad."

"She was our MOM, Ken. And we were never kids. Especially not after she disappeared."

"Left, you mean."

"Abducted, Ken."

Ken shook his head in disgust.

"I'm closing in on it."

"Jesus. Thad."

Thad held up his hand. His voice was mild. "Kindly do not question the evidence of my own eyes." He drained his beer, set it on the bar on top of a limp ten.

"Can I ask you something? Why? Is it because you think she'll come back?"

"I thought you of all people would understand. Jesus, *why.* Because *Mom didn't leave us.* She *loved*

52

us. She would have never left us alone with Dad. How can you not *know* that?"

Ken signaled the barkeep. "Vodka rocks. Make it a double."

"What a coincidence."

"What's that supposed to mean?"

"Your drink - it's the same as dad's. Chip off the old block, huh, Kenninator?"

Ken shrugged, but he'd been pissed. He couldn't believe Thad was still on about the fan man. After the joke Thad and his friends had played on him. After everything he'd done for Thad. After everything they'd been through.

"Let me guess, you know where Mom is." Ken said sarcastically. But Thad would not be drawn.

"You don't know anything, Ken. You just think you do. Me, I've been tracking activity for years now. And I do know some things. Like that Mom died in childbirth years ago." He swung off his stool, leaving Ken staring at him, open-mouthed.

"I'm going to walk back, catch some air. Maybe get an early flight back. I'll see you later."

It was the last time he saw Thad alive.

***

The summer he turned sixteen Thad began spending more and more nights away from home.

"Working," he grunted at Ken, when questioned. He said no more, leaving Ken to speculate what work required him to be out all night, coming home with twigs in his hair, dirt crumbling from his knees and elbows, camo paint on his face.

53

One night Ken woke to a headlamp shining in his eyes.

"Kenny. Hey, Kenny, wake up."

"Stop it, Thad. I have a test tomorrow." Ken turned on his side away from the light. The digital clock glowed 12:34.

"I know where Mom is."

Ken rolled back over and squinted up at Thad, a hand up to block the glare of the headlamp. Thad tossed something at the foot of Ken's bed; in the beam of his headlamp the red of the jacket and the green of the pants were like a CGI trick in a black and white movie. Ken's heart thumped strangely in his chest. It had been years since he'd seen this jacket, these pants. He touched them wonderingly.

"Where did you find these?" Even to his own ears, Ken's voice sounded excited.

"I'll tell you where she isn't - with some fuckin Argentinian ski instructor. Come on, get up. I got something to show you."

Ken dressed, pausing between pulling his shirt, pants and shoes on to finger the jacket in wonder and growing excitement. No use telling himself it was some other ski patrol jacket - it had her name patch and the thousand little details a mother's son would notice: the cigarette burn expertly patched with a tiny peace sign, the discoloration on the underside of the right arm where bleach spilled on it. The enamel pin of a unicorn was gone, but you could still see the hole in the jacket where it had once held fast.

Thad led them back into the canyon two miles from their cabin. The darkness was total, pressing hard against the pale white cones of light from their headlamps. Ken could hear rustlings as creatures skittered away from them through the brush, or paused to take their measure. It was the hour black bears were abroad, but when Ken began to whistle to give warning of their approach, Thad whirled on him with a finger to his lips.

"Quiet, big brother," he whispered - the same thing Ken had whispered to Thad the night their father burned their mother out of their lives. He shivered, only partly from the cold.

They veered off the trail, climbing a steep hillside toward the ridge. Something large and heavy sounding blundered away from them with a great snapping of branches. Thad froze for a second, hand in the air telling Ken to hold up; after a moment he continued the upward climb, Ken following. As they gained altitude a trick of the light made Thad seem to get larger, his shoulders broader, his legs moving powerfully, easily upslope while he, Ken was getting smaller and weaker, flailing in his brother's footsteps.

It was well after one when they slipped over the ridge; a bright half moon riding high in the sky like a ladleful of light. Was his Mom somewhere looking up at this same moon somewhere? Did she think of them? Ken thought not; even the good memories with Thad and Ken would be tainted by the stain of their father, like rancid balloons that when popped would rain down piss that stank of vodka.

They followed the ridge line for a half mile, shoes crunching over patches of snow still scattered here and there, thin and icy and sprinkled with pine needles. Ken was just getting ready to tell Thad he was turning back when his brother stopped abruptly. He took a pair of binoculars from his pack and another pair for Ken - expensive night vision goggles, what looked like Army issue. Ken pocketed his headlamp and strapped it on, intrigued despite himself.

Thad took a position on his stomach. After a moment, Ken lay next to him in dirt scrimshawed with ice, looking through the goggles in the same direction, more or less, as Thad.

The world swam into greenish, underwater focus. In the alien light the trees looked like ghosts of themselves. Turning his head toward a nearby scuffling in the leaves, Ken caught his breath. A four point buck stood less than fifty feet away from the spot where they lay. Ken could even make out the white blaze on its chest. The buck was looking in the same direction as Thad; Ken zoomed in to see its black nostrils widening rhythmically. It turned its head in their direction, its eyes glowing white orbs.

He felt Thad's hands on either side of his head, guiding the direction of his gaze. At the movement, the buck slipped away, making surprisingly little noise.

Where Ken's goggles were pointed, the ridge line that ran east-west along the northern lake shore abruptly jagged south. A dark mouth yawned on the hillside - a cave.

"Watch," Thad whispered.

They sat in silence for a while. Ken began to feel cold, the points of his elbows sinking into the snow and leaves and dirt. Then the tree next to the cave seemed to move; a piece of the trunk slowly split itself off from the rest of the trunk and dropped inch by inch to the ground. It stood so still that Ken lost it again, its shape blending with the dark trees around it.

It turned toward the mouth of the cave and made a gesture that made Ken's skin prickle with danger. Then the thing jerked upward out of his field of vision. He moved the binoculars around in frantic little circles but detected no movement, no man-shape.

"In the tree," Thad whispered.

He felt Thad's finger tilt the binoculars up, up. At last he found it, its alien eyes looking straight at him. There was keen intelligence in those eyes but nothing human.

A dewlap unfolded, spread a glowing fan beneath its chin. Ken felt his crotch go warm.

"I think it knows we're here," Thad whispered.

***

Ken skied as fast he dared, snapping glances upslope behind him to see if the thing followed.

Chelsea. She was probably headed back up the lift even now, snowboard dangling from one foot.

The thought prodded him faster down the mountain, even as he told himself it was all for nothing - she probably took the high speed lift all the way to the top. Or was still down at the base, chatting with ski patrol friends. Or even on her way to Bridgetender.

But the fear in his gut told him none of those were true. She was a natural, like Thad. A ski bum. She lived for long runs alone in the backcountry.

There was a time he skied as well as Thad, but that time, like their mother, was long in the past, like visiting a foreign country. He skied the chair line so he'd be sure to see her on her way up. The late afternoon snow mounded into moguls. The fall line was steep; he had to concentrate on his turns, keeping them tight but relaxed, his shoulders square with the bottom of the mountain, his knees bouncing. He went carefully and deliberately and without pause.

"Nice form!" The voice came from directly above him. Ken nearly crashed with the surprise of it, and a peal of laughter sounded - Chelsea riding the lift alone strapped into a Jones snowboard. Headed towards the Palisades. Just like that thing.

"Don't go," he yelled up at her. His panting snatched the power from his voice.

"See ya tonight!" she yelled, the chair moving inexorably upward.

He swept his arm toward the groomer runs farthest from the Palisades, farthest from where the thing disappeared, hoping she'd get the message *Go that way.*

She waved, the white of her smile still visible.

They were closing the gates to the automatic scanners for the lift. at the base. "I just saw a mama bear with cubs," he told the lift operator, panting. "Just over the ridge, on Palisades."

The operator radioed to someone - the same bored young man he had just pratfalled in front of Ken assumed.

"Hey Corey, any bear activity on Palisades ridge? Over."

"That is a negative, no bear activity, over," came the reply.

"Skier here says a mama bear and cubs headed Palisades way."

"That's a negative, no skier on Palisades for the last half hour," came the reply.

Ken felt his face burning. "I saw it from the lift," he said.

"Keep an eye out, warn all skiers," the lift operator radioed.

"Roger over and out," came the laconic reply. In the background, Ken heard, or thought he heard, the faint distant whoop of a woman's voice.

She'll be fine, he told himself. *That thing is twenty miles away by now.*

He tried hard to believe it.

***

He took a stab at cleaning up while he waited for Chelsea. In fact without all of the hunting and spying maps and gear, the place was downright spartan.

By six he was hungry so he ordered a pizza from Front Street. By the time he was on his second slice he knew she wasn't coming. His phone remained silent - no text, no voicemail. He figured it was just as well. It was not that he had his hopes up - He did, or was starting to. It was that she was a last link to Thad, as he'd been, unknown to Ken, a guy unsuccessful by most of society's measures but interesting enough to snag a hottie like Chelsea. He didn't want to get between that image of them, one in which Thad had been happy.

He finished washing his few dishes in the sink, his unshaven face reflecting back at him from the window. He snapped the light off and his reflection disappeared. The trees jumped into moonlit relief on the snowpack, sugar pines and white firs and the little quaking aspen still hanging on after all these years.

He still remembered planting it with his mom, her in her boho dress with the turquoise medallion around her neck, a floppy denim hat. Thad nearby in his bassinet. The big flower pot with the leggy red geranium. The aspen's yellow medallion leaves flipping this way, then that.

He picked up the military grade thermal vision goggles Thad left on the windowsill. A strange place for something so expensive. He held them to his eyes, looking out at the dark backyard. The creature was there, on the tree nearest the hot tub. It clung easily to the bark with webbed, claw-tipped hands and feet, stared at him with moonlight eyes. As Ken looked, a fanned fringe slowly unfurled around its head.

Ken felt his crotch go warm.

***

The cabin was looking good - if not sale-ready, at least less like the place of a crazy woods dwelling cryptozoologist (another word their Mom had taught them, meaning "bigfoot hunter").

When Ken arrived it was to find the walls of the cabin covered with topo maps and a photograph of a vast snow field, a dark figure standing at the edge of the woods. Thad had written a quote in stark black lettering in the immensity of sky above it *There is great power in stillness.*

The big farm table that seated eight had been covered with more maps, pages from books and articles from magazines. All of it shellacked right onto the surface of the table.

A pamphlet advertising night vision goggles, the text underlined in a careful thick red line jumped out at him:

Things only get revealed in the circle.
You can see reflections from very far away.
Bright lights are always blinding.

There were photos, some taken with an instamatic, others taken with a telephoto lens, blown up to 20x24. Ridgelines, dells of trees, steep snowy slopes dotted with boulders, post-its dotted with Thad's notes, each one dated. In each one of them, the thing shadowy or blurred.

The month after the visit in Chicago the pictures changed; Thad had a new camera, his onecaptured thermal images. There were two pictures of the thing with the same background, a natural cave with a copse of trees in front of it. In one picture there was an indistinct form, more manlike than not, at the bottom in Thad-print the words *night vis.* In the other picture, the thing glowed a bright shade of white, not in the least human. At the bottom Thad had printed *thermal cam.* Then, underlined: *warm blooded.*

In subsequent pictures the thing was blurred again. *Maybe spotted me - so fast!* Thad wrote on one, the thing's head turned toward the camera. *Stalking?* on another, where the thing clung to the

61

trunk of a tree easily as a beetle some thirty feet in the air.

Then the series, achingly clear, of two: the big creature with a much smaller creature, its anthracite eyes huge in the thermal image, its short, plaited tail almost cute.

Half brother/ Thad had jotted. Ken stared at that one for a long time, calculating. The little one would be a young adult now. Strong and agile. Curious?

There was a journal with dates and notations.

Sept 2012 *Signs it's around: no bears*.

November 2013 *deer remains...carnivore*.

May 2014 Lakewood Bowl *followed me at a distance stayed in trees. So fast.*

June 2016 *thinner, slower, weaker - sick?*

October: *took deer sausage left on rock plateau.*

It had been hard going, removing the turquoise medallion where it had been decoupaged to the table right at the spot their Mom would sit and watch them eat breakfast before school, keeping them giggling with her steady patter of nonsense but keeping it low while their dad slept off his hangover. Ken had to use a chisel and a blowtorch. It cleaned up nicely with a few applications of turpentine. He held the roundness, still cool to the touch, for a long time until it grew warm as the fire which had burned all her things.

Among all the detritus he found a sketch - a good one - of the ridge from that night. In the foreground, two boys lay on their stomachs, heads low. Behind them stood a buck, antlered head turned in the same direction the boys had fixed their binoculars. On the dark ridge, a white shape, as inhuman as it is indistinct. Ken looked at the sketch for long minutes, wishing that Thad had drawn the boys with faces visible.

Of course what the sketch was missing was the key detail of Thad's friends sneaking up on them when they came off the ridge into the canyon on a rutted snow machine trail. They were still wearing their night vision goggles which revealed the occasional flash of the bright eyes of small creatures and another deer, frozen at the sight of these alien intruders with their misshapen heads and huge protruding eyes.

Ken heard before he saw the three things running toward them from a side trail, whooping and growling from lumpen faces of pale glowing skin, cave-like mouths, eyeholes full of shadows and moonlight.

In terror Ken turned and was two steps into a full run when he slammed into Thad, who was running toward the grotesque things. For a confused moment the feeling was they had switched roles, that Thad was the big brother and he, Ken, the one who needed protecting was stronger than ever.

He lay on the path, stars exploding across his vision. The sound of laughter made him realize: the things were Thad's friends in silicone masks to look like Michael Meyers, Freddy Kruger and Jason Voorhees.

He yanked off the night vision goggles, gasping for breath. He could hear Thad talking to his friends, who were laughing fit to split themselves.

"Fuck off, you guys. Not funny, you fucking assholes. Fuck you." Jeering. *Pissed himself! Did you see his face?*

Thad's face leaning over Ken's, offering a hand.

Ken ignored it, got up. Pushed the night vision goggles into Thad's chest.

"Fuck you, little brother. Don't you ever bring up Mom's name to me again."

He fished out his headlamp, strapped it on and walked home, the laughter of Thad's friends like hyenas behind him. Hours later, he heard Thad come in, his footsteps paused outside Ken's bedroom door. There was a long silence.

"Ken?"

"Go to sleep, Thad." He could feel Thad debating silently, then creak down the hall to his own room.

They never talked about her again.

***

He saw the first MISSING sign at the Bridgetender, recognized her wide freckled smile instantly, probably because the headshot on the notice mimicked his picture of how he met her: grinning on a chair lift, with a patch of blue sky behind her.

He asked the bartender for his order of fish tacos and fries to go. He drank his beer and tried to watch the football game on the television but his eyes kept going back to Chelsea's bluebird grin. The bartender followed his gaze.

"A real shame," the bartender said.

"You know her?" Ken asked.

"Yep. Lotta guys knew Chelsea." He raised his eyebrows in faux regret.

"A lot of guys know me, too," Ken said. "What's the problem with that?"

"Well I think the *problem* is *obvious*," the bartender said, lifting an eyebrow toward the MISSING sign.

"So she didn't want to sleep with you, that it?" Ken asked. His tone was light but hummed with threat.

"I was only joking," the bartender said in a huffy voice and distanced himself from Ken. A waitress brought out his order in a brown paper bag. Ken wondered if the special sauce contained some bartender spittle.

***

Cindy the realtor stopped by while he was grilling on the back deck. A strong breeze had sprung up, carrying the smell of cooking meat down the creek path to the canyon. He'd already delivered the message he was moving in, but of course she'd want to stay in the game. She brought him a geranium as a house warming.

"Looks like you're getting ready for a party," Cindy said brightly, gesturing at the huge pile of steaks.

"In a manner of speaking," Ken said.

"So you're moving back!"

"At least until they recover my brother's body."

"Oh my," Cindy said, looking stricken with sympathy. Then: "When will that be, do you think?"

"This summer," Ken said, grimly satisfied at how easy it was for her to expose her ghoulishness.

"*Well* now, it will be quite a change from Chicago," she said.

"I used to live here, remember?" Ken told her.

"Oh that's right," she said. "Why did you move, again?"

"My mom was kidnapped and my dad died and I was finished raising my brother. Who has also died."

"Oh that's *right*. I'm so *sorry* for your loss. So much of it these days with the pandemic. A lot of people are selling and moving away, getting a fresh start. Cabins like this, with character, are just what many buyers from the Bay Area are looking for!"

Ken grudgingly admired her elliptical tenacity.

"My dad died of alcoholism in the master bedroom," Ken said conversationally. "My brother was killed illegally dynamiting Palisades Tahoe - a crime he planned at the dining room table."

"In a seller's market like this buyers overlook everything," Cindy said smoothly "Even murder, probably. Let me know if you want help staging it, when the time comes. I know a great local designer. I can send her over to do a walkthrough anytime, get some ideas."

"Well there's still the question of my mother," Ken said helpfully. He piled the cooked steaks into a foil pan and slung a fist full of salt over the top. Then he added another row of steaks to the grill. They were T-bones. He and Thad had loved T-bones. Good growth in a T-Bone, their dad always said. After their dad died, Ken cooked them weekly, even if it meant black beans and rice the rest of the week they had a by-God T-bone on Sunday. It probably did more to hold them together than all of their words combined, Ken reflected.

Cindy the realtor was still smiling but now it had an odd frozen quality to it.

"Isn't she the one they say ran off? With that foreigner?" She pronounced it *FOUR-inner*. Her voice tipped up in friendly malice at the end of each sentence.

"Ran off... or maybe abducted, some said. It happens, right? Like that girl on the MISSING poster down at the Bridgetender?" He looked at her pleasantly or so he thought, but Cindy took a step back. Her smile flashed forth, white and sweet as marzipan.

She's afraid of me, Ken realized.

"Oh yes well that's just awful if she is missing, though I hear she's probably just holed up with someone. Anyway, Honey, you have been through a lot that is for *sure*. A lot of people who've been through would never come home again. And here you are."

"Here I am," Ken agreed. "Just a chip off the old block." He laughed and Cindy took another step back. She didn't like him. She didn't want to lose the sale, but she didn't like him.

"Well alrighty then. You take care now. You have my card if... if anything changes."

"You take care now, too." He was just repeating what she said as she walked away but she flinched as if the sound of his voice was the warning cock of a rifle. She was practically running when she got to her car and though Ken thought "good riddance" he did not say it but instead smiled pleasantly and kept his hand lifted in a neighbourly goodbye as she backed out onto Lake Boulevard Drive, her tires screeching a little.

Now she'll spread the word that the Porter family was a straight flush: a violent drunk, a faithless slut, one son a Unabomber and now the other son, the fourth card flipped over and look at that, a guy who talks about murder and abduction and lives alone in the family cabin.

And she wouldn't be far wrong, he thought, looking around the south-facing bedroom upstairs. The one with bunks he and Thad shared as toddlers, before growing into their own rooms, was now his war room. The chase the same one Thad kept at over decades, with a different version of the same goal. The thing that took their Mom was as dead as their Mom was. But the son she bore it - the child that had inherited her green eyes - was not. The son that would lead him to Chelsea.

***

Late that night, like most nights, Ken leaned back against the edge of the hot tub on the back deck, looking up at a star-scattered patch of indigo sky where the tree crowns didn't touch. That was called crown shyness, his mother had told them.

Thad had kept the hot tub in good repair, tinkering with the motor and replacing the electronics board himself. He had underestimated his brother, Ken thought.

He lay soaking for a long time, long after the lights of neighboring cabins turned off for the night and the road was clear of traffic.

68

Sometimes - not often - he thought about that night with Thad, stalking the creature in its cave. The way it had turned to look at something in the depths, its peremptory gesture toward whatever it was looking at, a gesture that said very clearly: Stay. How their night vision goggles had not been strong enough to penetrate the mouth of the cave.

Sorry, mom, he whispered, tipping his longneck in the direction of the ridge.

He'd gone up there, of course. Thad had all the equipment - ropes, shoes, carabiners and pitons he needed to get up there, though it was tough going. The cave had long since collapsed, or been detonated. A sharp mineral smell permeated the air, thick and organic. But he never found even the smallest sign of her. Eventually he stopped going.

Back in Chicago he'd kept the door to her memory firmly shut and locked. But as he repaired the deck-boards she had walked and stood and danced on with her young sons - thoughts of her crowded in. The air was still cool, spring with a bite of winter, but the sun was warm and slanted into him as he sanded and sealed. And in the end it looked good: potted flowers, an umbrella table with chairs for eating outside when the weather warmed a bit more. A deck, he thought she'd approve of.

Just out of sight was the part Thad would approve of: floodlights mounted just under the roofline and motion-activated cameras hiding in the potted flowers, the chimney and drilled into the trunks of trees dotted with woodpecker holes.

When surprised or threatened they climb, Thad had noted on one of his Post-its. The sticky capture nets strung between the upper branches of the trees were barely visible, even with his head tilted back in the hot tub, staring up at the sky.

He'd lost weight since returning home, as if being pulled all the way back to the way he was right before he left for college. As if his body remembered how hungry he was all the time in his teens, actual growing pains keeping him up nights, his stomach turned into an unending pit of need.

His hands suddenly too big for the ends of his arms. Going hard in the snowpark doing tricks that made his blood run cold remembering, spinning like gods in the air until you were yanked back to earth, jaw clicking, neck snapping. His whole uncomplicated teenage American male life like countless teenage male lives around the earth, reduced to the twin engine cyclic forces of food and sex, food and sex. For a while there, it seemed he wanted only to be having one or the other and when he wasn't he couldn't think of anything else. Was there anything more predictable than a growing boy?

He tried not to think about what his mom had gone through, what Chelsea might still be going through.

He cooked outdoors three or four times a week, usually steaks and hamburgers with maybe a potato or corn for himself, piling the meat in a pan that he left first at the trailhead, then in the middle of the yard, lately on the table on the deck, a few feet from the hot tub. In all this time, no bears had come around to investigate, noses leading them to the pile of waiting meat. Not a single one.

It was getting close, then. Hanging around. Sometimes leaving the meat. But sometimes, taking it.

Without the bubbling of the hot tub jets (he never turned them on, nor the underwater lights) it was quiet but not silent; the night was full of small sounds. The reedy call of crickets. Insects chirruping. The soft intermittent query of owls. The scurry of chicories in the fallen pine needles, the snap of twigs sounding not unlike softly advancing steps, the almost imperceptible click of the camera. A smell of dirt and minerals. His fillings suddenly aching, tasting of metal.

With steam rising all around, he lifted the turquoise medallion till it covered the moon.

One Of Them (Thomas M. Malafarina)

1

The filthy, skeletal wreck of a man looked out from his hiding place at the edge of the dark pine forest, bordering   a cornfield. The massive evergreen trees stretched high into the sky and were thick and lush with needles, providing him the protective cover he required. Their scent, although quite pleasant, did little to mask the myriad of other much fewer desirable odors. Trevor managed to temporarily put the stench of rot and decay out of his mind as he had pressing issues to focus on for the moment.

His clothing hung from his bony frame like an extra-large flannel shirt dangling from a bent wire hanger. Had he been dieting and had successfully lost his desired weight, someone no doubt would have told him to get rid of his "fat dude" clothes and score some new lean, mean threads. However, that wasn't the case. Trevor hadn't been very heavy before everything happened and now he considered himself lucky to have what clothes he did have, let alone concerning himself with fashion. Besides, there was no longer anyone to impress with his clothing choices. Nor was there anyone to offer style advice. None of that nonsense mattered any longer. Almost nothing mattered to him any longer, outside of the simple act of staying alive for yet another day.

A cool autumn breeze blew in from the west, whispering its haunting refrain high in the pine boughs above him. There was a slight chill on that breeze, signaling the inevitable arrival of colder weather. It took Trevor aback for a moment, as he reluctantly had to face one particular fact he had been avoiding for weeks. At some point very soon, he would have to either find some warmer clothes and a better place to hide out, or else he would have to come up some way to relocate further south for the winter. He was going to have to do something before the severe cold arrived and by the feel of the chill in that breeze, he didn't have much time.

To take the risk and head south might be a better idea after all. Sure, the trip would be dangerous and the chances of surviving such a journey were slim. However, Trevor wasn't sure if he'd even still be alive when winter finally did come, regardless of where he was residing. nothing was keeping him where he was, no friends, no family, no Margaret, absolutely nothing. If he did decide to stay and somehow survive winter's deep freeze, he would likely end up dead shortly after that anyway. He couldn't avoid them forever.

Trevor knew that was an extremely frustrating and useless train of thought, which only succeeded in leading him into bouts of deep depression. In that state, he often found himself wondering if it was worth continuing, worth trying to survive day after endless day. Was it worth suffering through the cold all winter, with just the slimmest chance for survival, only to die at the whim of one or more of those horrible things come springtime? Trevor understood that this line of thinking was fruitless and counterproductive, but whenever the feeling overtook him, he couldn't help himself. Now that he thought about it, maybe this particular malaise was nothing more than an adverse reaction to that God-awful stink he dealt with day in and day out. He had been wrong and hadn't been able to put the foul stench out of his mind after all.

It was there. It was always there; the all too familiar reek hanging on the breeze like soot on a clothesline. It was a pall Trevor knew far too well but wished he didn't. The stink was a mixture of burnt wood, feces, rotten fish and the collective decomposing flesh of all humanity.

That odor had once been enough to turn his stomach and have him vomiting uncontrollably and it had done so many, many times previously. Now, however, after months of living with the vile stench, he had somehow become far too accustomed to it. That one simple fact troubled him in ways he couldn't quite explain even to himself. He had become so used to it he rarely, if ever, felt like tossing his cookies anymore. Then again, there were no longer any cookies for him to barf up anyway. His stomach was as empty as the White House and the halls of Congress were these days.

The thought of food had him staring longingly at the cornfield, not sure he could believe his good fortune. He had accidentally stumbled upon a field, thick with a crop of tall, healthy corn. How had they possibly missed it? As far as Trevor could tell, those horrible things were nowhere in sight, at least for now. In the shadowed darkness of the night, Trevor could see the tops of the tall stalks swaying in in the cool breeze.

Trevor remembered a country expression about corn stalks from back when he was a kid. It went

74

something like, "knee-high by the fourth of July." It was now early October, at least he believed it was October and this field was well beyond knee-high. There was enough corn in an area that size to keep him alive for months. That is to say if he had a safe way to cook the corn, which he didn't. However, Trevor wasn't thinking about that now; he was simply staring in awe at the rows and rows of ripe corn just waiting for harvest.

Trevor ha rightfully assumed such fields were gone forever. He had been sure he would never find such a near-perfect, unmolested crop again. Yet here was one, so close, he could almost reach out and pluck an ear from a stalk. A large plump looking ear was just a few short feet from his grasp. Maybe he should take it. He probably would have done so already had it not been for one fundamental fact. He understood he dared not reach out and steal even as little as a single ear of corn until he was sure beyond any doubt that they were nowhere around. Until then, as far as he was concerned, that cornfield might as well be on the far side of the moon. That was all because of them.

The corn appeared to be ready for harvesting, its many stalks sporting thick ears, but Trevor knew no one would be around to bring in this particular crop of corn. The farmer may have been there to plant the corn and keep it watered and fertilized initially, but that was months ago. The corn had grown without further intervention since then because that was how things worked; you planted seeds, some take root, it rains, and the corn grows.

However, this crop would not see a harvest. After all, it's impossible to run farm equipment when you're dead. Whoever the farmer had been who planted this corn, he was most likely among the millions and millions of the recently deceased. On the other hand, if the farmer wasn't already dead, he was probably too busy trying to stay alive to worry about bringing in any harvest, especially when there were so few if any humans still living to enjoy the fruits of his labor. However, Trevor was alive and he was standing just a few precious feet away from nourishment and he was starving.

His bloodshot eyes bugged out from dark-rimmed sockets and his skin clung to his skull. His hollow, sunken cheeks were a testament to just how much weight he had lost. He hadn't seen his reflection in months, but he knew he must be a dreadful sight based on the rippling of the rib bones he could see under his flesh. Then there was the constant exhaustion. He only had to do a few hours' work and he found himself needing to sleep. He suspected he would have to find some vitamins during his next supply run into the city, assuming he would be able to find the strength to do it.

The crescent sliver of the moon did its best to shine down on the field, but its meager light provided little illumination. Trevor couldn't see across the tops of the seven-foot-high stalks. He was looking for shadows, for movement, for any signs of them. He stood in absolute silence, not wanting to make even the smallest of sounds. He worried that even his ragged breathing might attract their attention. He needed to be sure the field was clean. He doubted it could be. In the first place, such treasure troves were never clean and in the second place, his luck simply wasn't that good. He couldn't hear a sound. Perhaps his luck had changed. Maybe this night fate would grant his wishes.

Then as if fate was waiting in the wings to crush what little remained of his already broken spirit and drive away every ounce of foolish hope, he heard it; the steady, distant, faint chomping sounds of them, the invaders. They had found the field and had begun chewing up the corn stalks. First, he heard one and then two, then the numbers started to grow as they always did. The chomping noises geo closer and gradually rose in volume. How many were out there now? Perhaps there were several dozen, a hundred, or more. He suspected many more than that by the ever-growing sounds of their relentless chewing.

Trevor cautiously backed up, pulling himself further into the dark recesses of the forest, feeling the thin pine needles brushing gently against the skin on the back of his neck. He knew he could not remain long where he was because they would attack the forest once they finished with the cornfield. They seemed to care little for the forest greenery but ate their way through woodland, searching for other planted fields.

A second later, he heard the sound of a twig breaking far off to his right. He turned his head quickly in that direction to see a large buck stepping out of the forest. It was a massive thing with a gigantic rack, likely a ten-pointer or better. Trevor was amazed at how majestic the creature managed to look, even though it was starving as severely as he was. He could see the deer's ribcage through its filthy mottled hide. The buck stagger-stepped out of the forest, heading toward the prize, waiting in the field. The creature seemed oblivious to the danger Trevor knew waited in the cornfield.

The chomping sounds ceased simultaneously. Then, like a sick and twisted version of a synchronized swimming event, large, shadowed bulbous heads began to arise from the cornfield to a height of more than twelve feet. Trevor was thankful for the night. He had seen them in all their horrifying detail before and felt the darkness was a blessing, protecting him from the horrendous visage.

The buck remained stationary, assuming what Trevor believed to be a fighting stance. The poor, pathetic beast was in no way prepared to fight anything, nor was he prepared for the inevitable death that awaited him among the savage creatures in the field. Perhaps the animal was starving to the point of hallucinating because it seemed only to care about getting an ear of corn. Trevor knew precisely how the buck felt. If his mouth wasn't so dry, he might be drooling at the thought of such a great feast as fresh corn. The deer took a step forward and stretched its neck outward to reach the elusive ear of corn. That was when all Hell broke loose.

First, Trevor heard a syncopated hum erupting from the hundreds of shadowy creatures in the field. It always seemed to be that way; the low buzz like a thousand insects, building up to a crescendo, after which all that remained was death and destruction. As the buck bit into the nearest ear of corn, a long greenish brown tentacle shot out from the cornstalks, followed by another, then another. They wrapped themselves around the struggling beast as they pulled him into the cornfield.

Within seconds, Trevor saw a shower of blood, hide and bone flying up from the field as the monsters tore the buck to pieces. The deer's shredded fragments flew through the air above the stalks, hurling from creature to creature in an orgy of bloodlust. They devoured the deer even though these creatures cared nothing for meat or flesh. They preferred to consume only vegetation. Regardless, their usually vegetarian diet did nothing to suppress their savage aggression, surpassing the most dangerous earthly carnivores.

For the briefest of moments, Trevor considered trying to snag an ear or two of corn himself during the confusion of the attack but realized any such attempt was futile and would likely end with his meeting the same fate as the deer. He had seen it many times before. Humankind had become as insignificant as an insect trampled underfoot. These creatures had a mission and humanity was expendable.

2

Trevor sat in the silence of his cave, a tattered blanket wrapped around him. It was cold, wet and dark, but the cave was the place he now thought of as home. He wondered if his other home still existed, the one from before everything went sideways. He supposed not. There had been so much destruction, so many dead, so much gone that he was sure his house couldn't possibly still be standing. If somehow it had miraculously survived, what did it matter? What did any of the possessions of his former life matter anymore? Everything he loved was gone. Everyone he loved was gone. The universe had seen to that. The creatures had seen to that.

As with his many previous bouts of depression, he felt himself slip-sliding into yet another chasm of darkness. He suspected seeing what had happened to the deer the previous night might have triggered this feeling of melancholy, but then again, maybe not. More and more often, he found himself sinking into darkness. He was helpless to stop himself from recalling what had happened. This train of thought eventually led him to think about Margaret. It always did. This particular malaise had seemed to wrap its black arms around him more frequently these days and had been doing so with increasing severity. He supposed it was a natural progression of sorts brought on by the hunger, the sleeplessness, complete solitude and the acceptance of the utter futility of his situation. This horrid existence was going to be his life for as long as he lived.

Trevor sat staring out at the tiny slit of an entrance to his cave. It was barely wide enough for him to slip through, even in his reduced physical state. However, that slit provided a level of security that suited him just fine. He could see the sun was rising out beyond the opening, which meant he must remain inside. It was treacherous enough to venture outside at night. It was suicide to do so in the light of day. These creatures ate ravenously around the clock. That was how it had been from the day they arrived.

He recalled how they had come so suddenly several months earlier, their thousands of massive disc-shaped crafts blocking the sun. It was so strange how the ships had appeared. One moment they weren't there; then the next, their ships filled the skies. It had reminded Trevor of science fiction movies he had seen as a boy, where aliens crossed into our dimension by using some sort of black hole or tear in the fabric of time and space. Their arrival was so unexpected and they had come in such incredible numbers none of the mighty armies of the world could have even hoped to repel them.

The hideous creatures that came down from the ships wore no armor, at least not in the traditional sense. However, they did have something like an invisible force shield, which protected them from humanity's tools of war. They carried no weapons. They dropped no bombs. They most certainly could kill and kill they did, by the billion.

As if having a monster rip you to pieces wasn't a horrible enough way to die, some people became nothing more than murderous flesh puppets for the creatures. Some of the monsters, the ones Trevor thought of as pack leaders, seemed to possess psychic abilities and could cause unsuspecting humans to see and believe whatever they chose. At least, that was what he felt in the beginning. Then after months of observations, he changed those presumptions.

From what Trevor had learned back then, it seemed that the alien forces divided themselves into tens of thousands of clusters, each consisting of several hundred creatures. Each cluster had a leader not only to control all the lesser creatures in its collection but one that communicated with other group leaders. Trevor wasn't sure, but he suspected that there were limits to how far away and how many group leaders could communicate in this way. But the number was irrelevant. According to this first theory, it took only a second for a group on one side of the world to relay its message to a group here in his backyard. It was Like a computer sending a signal across a worldwide network,

Later he learned more. Like all good scientists, he changed part of his hypothesis. He realized much too late this transference of signals didn't originate on the ground and pass from leader to leader. They were coming from whoever or whatever beings were up there in those ships. They were sending orders directly to the horrible, ravenous creatures on the ground. He had been correct about the psychic abilities of the so-called group leaders controlling the lesser drones, but he was wrong about them communicating with each other. All orders came down from on high.

To make matters worse, this psychic power from the controlling aliens took over the minds of the world's leaders. The creatures forced those leaders, in turn, to use the strength of their military to wipe out the human population. Instead of becoming a united front to battle the creatures together, every country on the globe went to war, not against the invaders, but against each other and in many cases against their own people. The aliens prevented the leaders from employing weapons of mass destruction such as nuclear, chemical, or biological. They needed to keep the crops safe from destruction. However, forcing the world's countries to fight each other allowed millions of soldiers and innocent civilians to die. As a result, the horrid creatures were unstoppable eating machines, essentially devouring all of the world's food crops.

They also somehow managed to place thoughts into the minds of millions of civilian humans, causing them to see each other as horrible alien creatures, as threats to their survival—this fabricated paranoia set man against man. No one understood this better than Trevor did. He had lived it and he had survived it.

Despite all the millions of deaths, it seemed to Trevor that these crop-eating creatures no longer went out of their way to hunt down and kill humans after their initial attacks. It appeared their assignment was to scour the planet and help themselves to all the crops. Granted, had he done as the buck had done the previous night, he knew they would have defended the corn crop they were eating and slaughtered him as well, but this was no longer their primary objective; consumption, was.

The crop-eating creatures possessed some sort of bizarre anatomical feature that allowed them to consume incredible amounts of crops, process them and pass them in the form of cylindrical greenish-yellow tubes. When Trevor first witnessed this happening, he thought they were simply passing waste material like feces. However, when he saw the skies blackened with fleshy flying things coming down from the ships by the millions to retrieve the cylinders and return them to their spacecraft, he understood these were not clumps of waste material but compressed food for those still above. He was confident the creatures were stocking the hulls of the ships with these cylinders to provide sustenance for future space travel.

These fleshy flying pooper-scoopers were pterodactyl-like in appearance with ten-foot-long gray-colored bodies and thirty-foot wingspans. Their wings were leathery, like those of a bat with the skin stretched tightly across an angular network of bones. They had massive flesh-covered legs ending in long talons with razor-sharp claws. Unlike anything Trevor had ever seen, these monsters had two additional sets of muscular arms with similar nails at the end of each bony hand. Their bodies were hairless and along their abdomens were several huge pouches, which the fliers filled with food cylinders. The most disturbing thing about these beasts was their faces. They had none. They appeared to have no heads whatsoever. At the place atop their shoulders, where one might expect to find a skull, was a low, glowing dome-like shiny yellow hump of flesh that vibrated and pulsed constantly.

Initially, Trevor thought these creatures were slaves to the aliens on the ground who served them by faithfully scooping up their cylinders and returning them to the ship. Then he realized things were more complicated than that. It took a while to sink in, but after many observations, eventually he began to realize these creatures weren't living beings at all, at least not in the sense that we as humans think of living, intelligent beings. They were biological machines, essentially mindless robotic things whose so purpose for existence was to fetch. He was uncertain about how the aliens in the ships controlled them, but he was sure they did.

After determining the nature of pooper-scoopers, Trevor began to wonder if these crop-devouring creatures on the ground were similar biological machines like the scoopers. He was sure their only purpose was to consume and process crops for the scoopers to take to the ship. However, if these creatures were machines, some were much more highly developed than others.

Once, while observing some of what Trevor considered lesser or drone-like crop-eating creatures, he noticed their synchronized, almost robotic movements. He believed their collective actions to result from some sort of hive mind. It was as though they all were sharing the same thoughts. If humans or animals got in their way during their feeding frenzy, the creatures dealt with them and did so quite savagely. Once the carnage was over, they went back into synchronized eating mode. Humanity and their counterparts in nature were little more than ants at a picnic.

If Trevor was right and neither of these species of monsters was the actual invaders but were nothing more than biological slave machines, he had to wonder who or what was up there in the ship. He suspected they might be creatures of incredible intelligence and psychic power, but were physically weak. He had visions of the tall, thin, bulbous head aliens depicted in sci-fi movies and referred to as 'grays.'

If that was what the beings in the ships looked like, it would explain why they had needed to create the hideous, monstrous creatures to do their dirty work. That would also explain the virtually mindless, syncopated constant devouring of Earth's crops over the past months. Trevor had no way of knowing if he was right or not, but he felt he might at least be thinking in the right direction.

In addition, hideous barely came close to describing the crop eaters. They were even more horrible to look at than the pooper-scoopers were. They were over twelve feet tall at full height, with no arms or legs. They appeared to be huge masses with layers upon layers of undulating skin, like mountains of rippling flesh. Trevor had seen how the giant monsters transported down to the Earth's surface. It had been some form of Star Trek-ian teleportation.

He didn't understand why the invaders used the robotic scoopers to retrieve the crops instead of simply "beaming" them up, but he suspected they must have had a good reason. Perhaps the purpose had been to keep the terror factor high because seeing the skies full of the pterodactyl-like monsters did indeed generate terror. Then again, maybe their teleportation was limited to the crop-eating monsters.

Dozens of thick, long tentacles streamed outward below these crop eaters' masses of blubbery flesh. At the end of each tentacle were a dozen or so long, fleshy, finger-like grippers. These tentacles and their grippers served several purposes. They were the monsters' sole means of ground propulsion. Trevor had seen with the buck the previous night and hundreds of times before, the tentacles also worked efficiently to grab and pull unsuspecting creatures to a gruesome death. Perhaps their most important purpose was to bring crops to the ugly bulbous head that sat atop the mounds of flesh.

The large balloon-like head was truly the creatures' most hideous feature, rising like a blister from their fleshy bodies. It had several giant wide mouths around its circumference, each equipped with hundreds of tiny, razor-sharp teeth, well suited for shredding anything that passed over them. The heads appeared to have no eyes, no noses, or ears, yet Trevor knew they could see, hear and smell exceptionally well; he just hadn't figured out how they accomplished this. Perhaps they had done so through sensors in their tentacles. It was yet another thing he didn't know.

He often wondered how many of those processed food cylinders plopping out of the backsides of these mountains of flesh contained the remains of dead, humans and animals. Did the beings in the ships even care? In his opinion, they didn't, because as he well knew, while the aliens systematically decimated the world's population, many formerly living creatures had passed through those horrible monsters.

He also had no idea how many humans still existed. He had to assume if he had managed to survive, then surely others of his kind had as well. After all, it wasn't as if he was exceptional regarding self-defense or survival skills. He was simply a regular everyday man who just happened to be still breathing. He had a suspicion that if he could just stay alive long enough, these creatures would finish raping the planet and move on to another one in some other galaxy. Then it would be up to him and any other survivors to take what would be a ruin of a planet, repopulate it and wait for it to regrow its crops. Perhaps they could help Mother Earth by planting seedlings if they managed to find any.

Maybe this was all just him being naive. Perhaps the aliens would decide to leave several thousand of their kind here as settlers to populate the planet with their species after the rest had moved on. For all he knew these beings might have done something like this on a hundred different worlds all over outer space. He supposed, if he somehow lived long enough, he would discover the answers to those questions.

Trevor thought again of how the aliens could plant ideas into most humans' minds and get them to see what they wanted them to see. For whatever reason, he seemed to be immune to their thought projections. He could only hope other humans had been as well. He believed that was why he was still alive, but it was also why his wife Margaret and his best friend Reggie were dead. When Trevor thought this, it always brought him mixed emotions. Of course, there was sadness, sadness for the death of Trevor's wife, Margaret, as well as the death of Reggie. If only he had gotten home earlier. If only he had taken Margaret away to safety. Even after all this time, Trevor felt like their deaths had been his fault, if not Margaret's, then just Reggie's. That was because Trevor had been the one who had put a bullet in his best friend's brain.

3

Trevor H. Stillwater and Reggie J. Ghent had been friends for as long as either of them could remember. It wasn't just because they were next-door neighbors, even though they were. It wasn't even because their parents were best friends and they were as well. It was just one of those things; they always got along and never fought or argued about anything. Even though they both had siblings, Reggie, two older sisters and Trevor, one older sister, and one older brother, the two were closer than they ever were with their own family members.

The pair grew up together, went to school together and eventually graduated from high school together. Things changed briefly when the boys went to different colleges far from each other. They drifted apart during the four to five years it took them to complete their higher education. They kept in touch when they could, usually over social media, but once they found girlfriends, that contact dwindled to nothing as well. After college, both boys returned to their parents' homes in Schuylkill County, Pennsylvania, to live rent-free for a while until they paid off their student loans.

Strangely, they hadn't run into each other since initially moving home. Neither of the young men had reconnected; they were busy trying to find jobs while maintaining long-distance relationships with their demanding girlfriends. Unfortunately, their girlfriends had no intention of settling down and raising a family in Pennsylvania. Both women insisted on getting wedding rings very soon and relocating their future husbands to what they considered more civilized parts of the country. When neither Trevor nor Reggie gave in to their constant barrage of nagging, they both received 'Dear John' texts and that was the end of that.

Unbeknown to each other, one weekend both young men ended up in the same local watering hole with plans to drown their sorrows. Trevor had looked up from his third Tito and Sprite to see Reggie guzzling down a mixed drink of his own. Reggie looked up and saw his old friend, the years melted away.

The two picked up their friendship as if all the things that happened during the previous five years were insignificant. They continued to be friends for many years to follow. They both eventually met and married twin sisters, which helped to make that close bond even closer. They were each other's best men during their double wedding ceremony.

They purchased and built new homes in an up-and-coming housing subdivision outside of Yuengsville, right next door to each other. Since they had married sisters, they were together for all family events. Although neither couple had children, they were looking forward to starting families and having their kids grow up together. It looked as if no force on Earth could end their friendship. Then the skies went dark with alien spacecraft.

The day the creatures arrived, Trevor was in Philadelphia at a seminar in an elegant high-rise office complex in center city. Like everyone else, when word of the strange objects blocking the sun spread, he ran from the office building out into the streets to join thousands of others who were standing and looking up into the skies, mouths agape, staring in awe. Who could blame them?

They were witnessing the sort of historic phenomenon they could have previously only imagined. Even the sci-fi books and movies they had all grown up with never did anything to prepare them for what they were witnessing.

Then, without warning, people looked away from the spacecraft hovering high above them and instead began looking at each other strangely. At first, Trevor didn't know what was happening or what to think. He felt fine. Why was everyone else looking at each other with such bizarre expressions? That question only had time to linger in Trevor's mind for a moment or two. That was until he saw a man standing three feet away from him, reach out his arms and plunge his thumbs into the eye sockets of another man. Blood streamed down the man's cheeks as his eyeballs popped like squashed grapes. The attacker was screaming, "You're one of them! One of them!"

Seconds later, off to his left, he heard a woman shouting, "You're one of them! I know you are!" She was grabbing hands full of another woman's hair and slamming the victim's head against the side of a brick building. Trevor's stomach lurched when he heard the poor woman's skull crack open. She slid down along the side of the building, an left a crimson soupy stain dripping down the bricks.

Trevor started to slowly back away as all around him he saw people trying to kill each other with whatever weapons they might have available. All the while they shouted slightly different versions of the same thing. They were accusing each other of being "One of them" and subsequently tearing each other to pieces. For whatever reason,

Trevor knew he wasn't experiencing the same strange paranoia as everyone else around him was. As he backed into the atrium entrance of the office building, he saw a few others who seemed as confused as he was. They were not affected either, at least not yet.

He made eye contact with a woman he recognized from his seminar and realized she was still normal like him. He started to head in her direction with the hope of getting to her, but he never got the chance. He heard someone screaming, "You're one of them!" as a wild man came in from the mob brandishing a long piece of metal rebar, wielding it like a long sword. It connected firmly with her skull and she fell dead on the ground. Then he turned to Trevor and, with the eyes of a lunatic, shouted, "You're one of them!"

Others inside suddenly began shouting at the intruder and moments later, at each other. Soon everyone in the office building was at each other's throats. The atrium was seventeen stories tall and within seconds, bodies began falling from the upper levels like rain as they crashed to the ceramic atrium floor and exploded into pieces. Trevor understood he was no safer inside the building than he was outside.

He saw a long piece of metal one of the crazies must have dropped during the carnage. The end of the thing dripped with blood and brain matter. Trevor grabbed it by the relatively clean side and began swinging it at anyone who came at him. He had no idea how many heads he cracked that day or how many arms and legs he had shattered. Nor did

Trevor know how many of those same crazies were still alive. He didn't care.

Fortunately for Trevor, the hotel he was staying in was just a block or so from the office. He fought his way back to the hotel, stealing occasional glances upward to the hovering discs as he swung his weapon at anyone in his path. When he reached the hotel, he ran to the parking garage and his car. He didn't bother going back to his room for his things. Anything he had brought with him was as useless as the training he had received earlier that morning. Trevor knew that self-defense training which, unfortunately, he had none, had suddenly become a far more critical skill than any other had.

His car was on the top floor of the garage. Trevor didn't bother with the elevator, taking the stairs two or three at a time. He, fortunately, didn't meet up with anyone in the stairway. By the time he reached the top floor, he had barely enough breath left to stand up straight. The area was empty of people and open to the sky. That was when he got his first good look at the alien spacecraft.

They were elliptical and more expansive than a football field. He was sure they must have had a curved top, but from where he stood, it appeared the bottoms were completely flat and smooth, with not a single sign of motors, drives, or any means of propulsion. He stared on in amazement as a beam of glowing white light, brighter than anything he could imagine, shot from the bottom of one of the ships. It projected onto the street below. Out from the beam lurched one of the most hideous creatures Trevor had ever seen. It was one of the monsters he would later learn devoured crop fields by the acres. He wondered what it was doing in center-city Philadelphia.

Soon Trevor had his answer as the monster shot out tentacles and began grabbing people and slamming them to the ground as quickly as a child might kill an insect. All the while this was happening; the people around the city were screaming and killing each other. Trevor looked on in shocked amazement as more beams of light shot down from the crafts and soon dozens if not hundreds of the creatures were grabbing humans and tearing them to pieces, dismembering them with the ease of a child ripping a paper to pieces.

He had only one choice. He had to get out of the city. He had no idea how he might accomplish this, but he had to try.

4

Thinking back to that day, Trevor was still unable to piece together exactly how he had managed to escape. It was all a chaotic blur to him. He had flashes of memories, fragments so vague he wasn't sure which events had happened at all and which his mind had fabricated to fill in some of the holes.

He remembered getting into his car and driving down through the parking garage and out into the street. He couldn't recall encountering any crazies in the garage on his way down. This recollection was where things were confusing. He had made it out of the city, had traveled the Schuylkill Expressway and eventually made his way back to Schuylkill County. Somehow he had avoided death from the aliens as well as the insane mobs fighting in the streets. He suspected he must have had to run some people down to escape. He only hoped they weren't innocents but people intent on killing him.

When he got back to his home, Trevor saw significant dents in the front of his car, as well as blood smears and clumps of hair stuck in the damaged areas. There was also one other thing he had found on the front seat next to him. It was a loaded handgun.

"Where the hell had that come from?" he wondered. He didn't even own a gun. Then he had a few scattered images of a police officer lying in a pool of spreading blood and a hand, his hand, lifting a weapon from the street. He couldn't recall hitting the cop or anything else, but the gun was here, so something had happened. Perhaps someday he'd remember if he lived long enough, but for the moment, he did not.

He pulled into the street of his subdivision which was dark. He was surprised to see there were none of the giant ships hovering. Yuengsville was a city but not one the size of Philadelphia. It seemed like the invaders were targeting large metropolitan areas first, so he was safe, at least for now. He couldn't recall seeing any during his trip home either. Then again, that part of his journey was as vague and spotted as the rest of it. He pulled into his driveway, opening his automatic garage door as he did do. The garage door worked; that meant he still had electric power. He wasn't sure, but he believed Philadelphia had been in a blackout state when he left.

Trevor got out and tucked the revolver into the back of his pants under his belt. He had no idea what he was doing, and for all he knew, he might very well be in danger of blowing his butt to pieces. Trevor quickly hit the garage door *close* button and raced into the house to see if his wife was safe. He found Margaret asleep on the sofa in the family room with the television on, but the volume turned down.

Trevor glanced at the clock on the family room wall and saw it was now 9:07 pm. He recalled first seeing the flying disks in Philadelphia around 12:30 and had likely left the parking garage by 1:30. Under normal circumstances, it might take two and a half hours to get home from Philly. That would only make it 5:00. Although he still had no recollection, it must have taken him four additional hours to return home.

Trevor suddenly felt a strange sensation beginning in the pit of his stomach, as if someone was playing bass-driven music through a giant subwoofer. He felt the hair on his arms and the backs of his hands stand on end. The lights in his living room began to flicker. He knew immediately what it was and could only hope he was wrong, but of course, he wasn't.

It was them, whatever sort of alien invaders they were, up there in the skies, above his town, above his home. They were here and Trevor knew what would happen next. He watched his wife sleeping on the sofa,

he noticed her leg twitch as she slowly came awake. Instead of seeing the welcoming face of his loving wife, he was looking into the eyes of a stranger and not just any stranger, a hostile stranger.

"You! You're one of the!. Oh, I know you are!" she bellowed.

Trevor pleaded, "No, Baby, please. Look at me. Honey, it's me, Trevor. I'm your husband."

"You're not my husband! You're one of them!" ade shouted as she walked over to the kitchen island and pulled a huge knife from the cutlery block. She turned and held the knife in front of her, pointing directly at him. She started to shout, "You're one of ...", but the sound of someone breaking down the kitchen door at the back of the house interrupted her cry. She turned at the sound. Standing in the entrance to the living room was Trevor's best friend, Reggie, wielding a baseball bat.

It was then Trevor saw that although technically it was Reggie standing there; it wasn't the same Reggie he had known all his life. This Reggie wore pajama pants and a white "wife-beater" undershirt with no socks or shoes. It was far too generous to call the tee shirt white considering it was soaked crimson with blood. Trevor knew the blood belonged to Reggie's wife.

"You're one of them," Reggie shouted at Margaret as he swung the bat, striking her on the side of the head so hard that her neck snapped with a sickening crack, killing her instantly.

"Noooooooo!" Trevor shouted as he reached into his belt, retrieving the gun he had confiscated earlier during the chaos in Philadelphia. He pointed it at Reggie and without taking even a moment to think, he pulled the trigger and kept doing it long after the last bullet had left the barrel. Reggie would have neither known nor cared, as the very first bullet had entered through his left eye and blown out the back of his skull.

5

Trevor now sat alone on the floor in his cave, staring out into the fading daylight. He must have dozed off for a time because the last memory he had was of the morning sun coming through the cave entrance. He was miles from Yuengsville, having fled on that fateful night, taking up residence in Mother Nature's version of a Motel 6 somewhere in the mountains outside of town.

He was still thinking about the cornfield he had seen the previous night and fantasized about how a fresh ear of cooked sweet corn might taste right about now. But he knew he was only fooling himself. Even if he had somehow managed to grab an ear of corn the previous night, what would he do with it?

There was no electricity, not that he had a stove in the cave anyway. He could never risk building a fire because the smoke would give away his location. He hadn't eaten anything requiring cooking in months. What little prepackaged food he had brought with him he ate cold and now almost all of that was gone, even though he had put himself on strict rations. Trevor didn't want to get to the point where he had to start trapping small animals again since the last time he had tried it, he had failed miserably. Any animals he had managed to catch he had to eat raw. As a result, he had

98

determined that the last experiment was a complete failure.

He looked into the red and white plastic Coleman cooler he used as a makeshift refrigerator, that is to say, one without any ice. Inside was a quarter of a Tastykake butterscotch Krimpet and a few sips remaining in the bottom of a bottle of spring water. The cake remnant had been waiting for him for three days and this was the last of his water. He was most definitely at the end of his rations now. Trevor knew by the evening he would have to abandon his cavern hideaway, if not permanently, then at least for a while, especially if he decided to head south. The cave may have provided him much-needed sanctuary, but it couldn't magically make food appear, especially food that he could eat without the need to cook it first.

Trevor released a frustrated sigh of resignation. It was possible, if not probable that he could end up dead this night. However, he had no choice; he had to go into the city. He had to go to Yuengsville and find food and, even more importantly, water. If he were killed, at least he would have died trying. He would wait just a bit longer until the sun was down. He kept his eyes trained on the thin slit of the cave opening. It wouldn't be long now. That was when he heard the sound of bushes rustling outside.

Maybe it was a small deer or a feral dog or cat. There were hundreds of them roaming the area. Trevor recalled the unpleasant memory of how he had killed small game on occasion but eating them raw had proven beyond repulsive. He had even tried baking them in the hot sun on a sheet of metal from an old car, but all the meat did was rot. He had found it teeming with flies and maggots after just a few hours. Maybe the noise wasn't a small animal. He recalled occasionally hearing the distance howling of packs of wolves or coyotes or feral dogs. Trevor supposed the noise he was hearing could be just about anything, even one of them. He hoped it wasn't.

If it was one of those creatures, he was probably a dead man. The opening might be too small for them to crawl through, but their long tentacles could easily reach in and pull him out. Trevor supposed it would also be possible for the beings inside the ship to transport one of the creatures inside his cave. There wasn't much room inside and such an attack would kill him instantly. Hell, it might even be possible for the creatures in the ships to transport him from the cave. The truth was, he had no idea exactly what all these creatures were capable of doing.

His muscles tensed as he watched the cave opening with increasing dread. Then he saw it, the shadow of one of those God-awful monsters passing by the cave entrance. Because of its enormous size, only the creature's squirming tentacles below the gelatinous undulating flesh were visible. Trevor sat stock-still, sweat beginning to drip down his brow and collect in his armpits. He prayed the creature would continue to pass by. That was when it stopped.

With absolute terror, Trevor watched helplessly as one long slimy tentacle oozed into the cave opening, like a snake slithering along the ground. He pressed himself tightly against the back wall of his small makeshift home and held his breath, trying desperately not to make a sound. The tentacle seemed alive as a separate, sentient creature unattached to the crop-eating beast. It raised and lowered its hand-like end, sniffing the air. It appeared to scan the area for what? Was it looking for crops to consume, or was it seeking survivors?

Trevor was still, his heart thumping so loudly in his chest he wondered why the searching tentacle hadn't sensed it as it moved about the tiny cave. He had a knife nearby but knew any attack he might attempt on the creature would be futile. For starters, the monster had many other tentacles. In addition, if there were one of those monsters outside, there would be hundreds. Any attack he made would instantly become the knowledge of the entire herd. If things were as Trevor suspected they were, this probing tentacle was transmitting its findings not only to its owner but to the rest of them.

He pressed himself tighter against the cave wall, wishing he could somehow pass right into it. He closed his eyes like a terrified child hiding under his covers to escape the boogeyman. Then, he sensed something nearby, something very close to his face. Trevor slowly opened his eyes just a crack and, in the darkness of the cave, he saw the hand-like end of the creature's probing arm just inches from his face. The tentacle performed an elegant ballet, like a cobra hypnotized by the music of the snake charmer's pungi.

His hand felt something cold near his fingertips and realized it was the butt of a gun. It was the 38 revolver, which he had found that first day in

Philadelphia. He knew it would be useless against the creatures, but if he had to...

What Trevor had thought were the monster's fingers were a dozen or more tiny tentacles. Each of them wriggled about in the air in front of his face. Some translucent slime coated the appendages, which appeared to have thousands of thick hair-like follicles.

He slowly and carefully lifted the gun to his temple. He wouldn't let these monsters take him alive. The truth was he didn't think he had any desire to die. No matter how bad things got, no matter how lonely and depressed he felt, he was confident he couldn't take his own life. But if he had to decide between death by his own hand or being torn apart by those Godforsaken monsters, he knew which choice he had to make.

The stench of the thing was dreadful, like a crate of fish rotting in the hot sun. Trevor was so thankful he had chosen not to eat that last morsel of cake, for just the thought of doing so combined with the stench of the creature made his stomach want to rebel.

Trevor managed to keep his increasing need to vomit at bay using willpower he wouldn't have imagined he possessed. His finger tightened on the trigger. He had made his peace and felt assured that since the invasion started, he had done everything in his power to stay alive. If this was how he was to die, then so be it. He had fought the good fight and had a successful run. Now he was hungry, thirsty and exhausted, not to mention depressed and frustrated.

Trevor held tightly to the trigger of the gun, closing his eyes once again, ready for the end to come. He was waiting for the first touch of the horrible alien tentacle, but it never came. That was when he heard the sound of something being dragged along the ground. He opened his eyes again to see a shadow of the tentacle retreating from the cave. He couldn't believe his luck; the thing was going away.

Slowly, taking great care to remain silent, Trevor released a breath he seemed to have been holding for eternity and lowered the gun from his head. The slimy arm had moved entirely out of the cave now and he could see shadows of more of the creatures passing by. It hadn't detected him. How was that possible? Why had it not known he was there?

Then Trevor realized it must have something to do with his immunity to their psychic suggestions. The creatures must not have the ability to sense his presence. That is to say, as long as he was standing perfectly still and only breathing in tiny silent breaths, they didn't seem to be able to. Trevor was sure that if he were walking or moving in any way, they would sense him. This little tidbit of information might prove to be helpful in the future.

If his earlier assumptions were correct and the results of that tentacle's investigation went along whatever strange telepathic network these monsters used, there would be no more tentacles probing his cave this night. Trevor waited until the last shadow passed his cave entrance. Then he waited some more. When he was confident the creatures had moved on, he headed out into the night to begin his quest for food.

6

Trevor headed in the opposite direction from that taken by the creatures. They were looking for crops he was heading to the city. He carried a large canvas backpack which he hoped to fill with food and water. If he were lucky, he might find a bicycle he could use to speed up his transportation. He had acquired one on a previous run and it served him for a while until it eventually fell into disrepair. Trevor was not very mechanically inclined and lacked the skills to do even the simplest repairs.

He knew he might be able to find a car or truck with the keys still in the ignition, but the noise from the engine was likely to bring him the sort of attention he didn't need. In a world now completely free of the typical sounds of civilization, the noise of even the quietest motor would become like the roar of a jet engine. If he could find a bicycle and travel by night, he believed he could reach Virginia in a few days. Then he would continue south for several weeks until he was far enough, so he no longer had to fear the winter's cold. Yes, there would be spacecraft and yes there would be creatures, especially in the fertile southern farmlands, but Trevor had gotten good at avoiding both. He believed he could make it if he could just first find food for his immediate needs then find enough supplies along his journey.

He walked on into the night, keeping his eyes and ears open for trouble. As he approached the edge of what had been the small forest where he had hidden in the previous night, Trevor was shocked to see a swath cleared in the forest about one hundred feet wide, resembling a pole line that stretched for miles. He knew what it was; he had seen it before. It was a path in the forest the monsters had made as they attempted to pass through in search of more fields. They didn't seem to want to consume forests, but as he knew, they could do so if it became necessary.

Trevor looked up into the night sky, surprised that he didn't see a single disc hovering anywhere in sight. He understood they could still be up there but maybe too high to see. Even if the ships weren't there now, they could appear in a millisecond as they had done that first day when they arrived. He suspected most of that had been for pure shock and awe value. With most of the human population decimated, there was no need for psychological theatrics.

He thought about what he had just said in his mind, "Most of the human population." He honestly did believe that even though he hadn't seen another living human in more than two months, there still might be a chance he could encounter survivors like himself. He wanted to believe and he needed to believe. He gripped the handle of the club he carried. It wasn't much of a weapon, but it was safer and quieter to than his gun. After what he had nearly done to himself in the cave, Trevor figured it was better to keep the gun at the ready as a last resort. The club would have to be his primary choice of weapons.

On the one hand, the club would be useless against any monsters, but then again, so would the gun. He could use the club to protect himself from any human crazies he might encounter. This made him wonder. If he did meet another human, would they be truly human, or would the invaders have altered their minds and made to see him as one of them? He suspected he would find out before too much longer.

Trevor chose not to walk through the cleared area but to stay to the surviving forest edge, out of sight and hopefully out of danger. He walked for what seemed like an hour before he got to the Southeast border of the city of Yuengsville. It was as he suspected, in complete darkness; there was no electricity, no power. Then again, there hadn't been any electricity since the day those dreaded invaders arrived. Perhaps they had used some sort of electromagnetic pulse generator to kill all the power. Trevor didn't know if such a thing was possible. Then again, three months ago, he never would have believed that what had happened to his world was possible.

He navigated only by the limited amount of moonlight available and carefully made his way through the side streets and alleys of Yuengsville, searching for former businesses he suspected might have food. After a few moments, he saw the familiar sight of a once-popular convenience store chain. It sat on a corner next to an alley, intersecting a street.

He carefully approached the building, being sure to stay in the shadows. He was listening for the sounds the creatures made, although it was apparent, they had been here and gone a long time ago. He was also listening for the crazies, as they were as dangerous to him as the invaders.

He slowly approached the front door and took one last look around before risking turning on his flashlight and pointing it into the gloom of the abandoned market. As he opened the door, an invisible cloud of vile reeking stench hit him in the face like a baseball bat swung by a major league home run king. He heard what sounded like the buzzing of a million insects as a massive swarm of flies as black as the night itself rose from the floor of the place. Trevor could feel hundreds of them slapping against his face.

He closed his lips and eyes tightly, stepped back outside and slammed the door shut. He heard the ticking sound of scores of the creatures slammed themselves against the glass in the door.

Trevor batted away the few dozen flies which had followed him out the door. He bent over at the waist, sure he was about to lose that last bit of cake and water he had eaten before leaving, but soon the feeling passed. He thought it ironic how the foul air of the world now seemed fresh compared with the pall inside that store. He had recognized that stench. It was the reek of the dead. He had no idea how many corpses lay rotting inside that building, but he believed there had to be quite a few to attract so many insects and create so much stink.

There was also food there and he needed to get to it. Anything not vacuum-sealed or in cans would have fallen victim to rot, insects, vermin, or all three. Trevor decided the best thing to do was to wedge the door open to try to get rid of some of the foul smell and hopefully some of the insects as well. He found a wedge of wood in a corner outside the store and, holding his breath, quickly opened the door, shoved the wedge under it then ran across the street. He hid out of sight in an alley between two buildings. It gave him a decent view of the store. He found it incredible how he could still smell the stink of the rotting corpses across the street.

After about two minutes, he heard the droning buzz of what sounded like a million insects. He stared through the minimal light from the moon and could see a cloud of flies, darker than the night, swarming out the opening. Trevor hoped they weren't just curious about the disturbance and were leaving for good. When he was about to leave his hiding place and head back to the store, he heard a series of deep guttural growls coming from the side street next to the store, directly across from him. He ducked back into the darkness of his alcove.

7

The first thing Trevor saw were two glowing amber eyes, low to the ground, coming out from the blackness of the alley. Soon the rest of the creature was visible and initially, Trevor thought it might be a wolf. But as the beast entered the light, Trevor saw it was a huge dog. An extremely large dog, perhaps a German shepherd mix and something even larger, like a Mastiff. It stood at least four feet tall to the top of its muscular back. Its head was massive and its eyes were focused and malevolent. The thing's mottled fur had large patches missing. Scars, wounds and dried blood covered the hound.

Its mouth hung open, revealing many large, deadly teeth, perfect for tearing flesh.

The beast was not alone. Five more sets of those wolfish red and yellow eyes followed it out of the alley. Although these dogs all looked dangerous, it was apparent the first one was their leader. They were a pack, a hunting pack. Trevor hadn't encountered such a group before, but sometimes at night he would hear howling in the distance and imagined troops of feral dogs moving about, scavenging for food. He reached into his backpack and took out the revolver. He had no desire to use it out of fear of attracting the aliens, but if he had no other choice than use it, he would.

He held tightly on the gun's grip as the dogs made their way toward the store. They were all battle-scarred with matted and torn fur. They got closer and one of the beasts, a hideous monster with a tattered ear and a missing left eye, stopped, turned in Trevor's direction and began sniffing the air.

"Oh no," Trevor thought, "He can smell me. How the Hell can he still smell me with that god-awful dead stench everywhere?"

Trevor had been right; the creature had smelled him, albeit a very small amount.

The dog took a single step in Trevor's direction, perhaps attempting to home in on his scent when the big dog leading the pack released a deep guttural growl. Obediently, the one-eyed dog took his place back in the formation. Yet every few seconds the dog would turn its head toward Trevor, sniffing the air. A dozen more dogs joined the original four at the sound of the lead dog's howl. Although not as big as the four scout dogs, these others looked every bit as wild. Trevor could see they were the females of the pack. Several of them were pregnant. By the look of the animals and how they moved together, they had already been a feral, working, hunting pack long before the world fell apart. Now their hunting lands had expanded to include the entire country.

The large male dogs guarded the open door, the females went inside. Trevor heard high-pitched squeaking sounds coming from the store as hundreds of giant rats began running out.

Trevor saw the stream of rodents heading straight for the same alley where he was hiding. He pressed himself against a brick wall and, like the previous day in his cave, he held his breath and closed his eyes. He could hear the smattering of hundreds of tiny feet scratching against the street as they ran past him. He cringed and practically screamed when several dozen of the pestilent creatures ran across his feet, brushing against his ankles. The feel of their bristly fur scratching against any exposed areas made his flesh crawl and the hair on the back of his neck stood on end.

After a few seconds, which seemed like hours, the rats were gone. Trevor heard the sound of something dragging along the ground. He opened his eyes again and, looking over at the store, he could see one of the female dogs walking backward, dragging a half-eaten corpse with her. The dog's jaws locked around the poor dead soul's skull as she pulled the already mutilated corpse out into the alley. Soon another dog came out with a corpse, followed by another, then another. Trevor could only determine male corpses from females by the tatters of clothing remaining on the bodies.

He imagined what might have likely happened to them to cause their demise. They were probably out shopping, perhaps stopping by to get a cup of coffee or a soft drink; maybe picking up some milk or a loaf of bread, when the spacecraft appeared overhead. A few seconds later, they would have seen each other as monsters and they would have begun killing each other.

After numerous trips in and out of the door, the dogs had nine rotting carcasses littering the street. Trevor's heart sank when he noticed two of the bodies were smaller than the rest. Children. One of them was dressed in filthy tattered jeans and tee shirt and one in the remnants of a blood-soaked pink dress. There was something about those two tiny bodies, their fragility and their innocence, which made Trevor feel even more despondent than he had ever felt before.

All the dogs stood silently, staring hungrily at the remains, apparently waiting for permission from the lead dog to begin. The alpha dog grunted once and the males began feasting, tearing strips of remaining gray, rotten flesh from the corpses. The females waited patiently for the signal telling them it was time to start eating. When the males were finished, they backed away and, with another grunt from the lead dog, the females began to tear into the remains.

Trevor had no idea how long he stood waiting in the shadows for the dogs to finish, watching them rip the bodies apart, consuming them. Each time he heard the cracking of bone as the beasts went for the marrow, he felt like a piece of his mind was cracking right along with it. Probably not more than a half-hour or so passed, but it felt much, much longer. To Trevor, this feast of flesh had become more than something ghastly to witness; it had become symbolic of what had happened to his world, to humanity.

The one-eyed dog that had concerned Trevor so much seemed to have forgotten about him. It never sniffed the air or looked in his direction again. Trevor assumed the stench arising from their savage feast was such that nothing but the stink of decomposing flesh and rancid blood filled the animal's nostrils.

After a time, the massive leader lifted his snout and let loose with a blood-curdling howl that echoed in the confines of the street, reverberating off the large abandoned brick buildings. Soon the other males, followed by the females, joined in. Trevor pressed his back against the building again, closing his eyes and covering his ears with his hands, trying fruitlessly to block out the sounds.

Not for the first time since all of this alien horror began, he wondered how much more of the insanity he could take before his mind finally snapped. There was now as much to fear from creatures of his world as those monsters from space. In the beginning, he had considered himself lucky to have survived for as long as he had. However, more and more these days, he wondered if he wouldn't have been better off dying early on. He might be with his beloved wife Margaret and his friend Reggie if that happened.

Trevor felt something cold against his right ear and realized he still held the revolver in his hand. How easy it would be for him to simply press the barrel against his temple or place it inside his mouth, feeling the chill of the metal against his tongue. One simple squeeze of the trigger and it would all be over; no more hunger, no more fear, nothing but peace. He no longer feared Hell as he was living in a Hell worse than any he had ever imagined. Why not just do it and free himself at last?

Trevor realized the howling had stopped. He looked into the street and saw the dogs' backs as they departed down the same alley they had entered. He tucked the revolver back into his pocket and began to cross the street to head into the store. He walked over the scattered bones of the dead, doing his best not to look down at the carnage. He tried to ignore the sounds of the broken bones crunching under his feet. He did his best not to think about the tingling feeling which seemed to radiate up through his shoes, along his legs and up into his brain. Then he saw the scattered remains of the two little ones.

Trevor tried desperately to put the image out of his mind and entered the store. He saw, to his surprise, an adult-sized bicycle leaning against a wall. It seemed to be in working order and had a wire basket on the front and several leather saddlebags on the back. Store employees must have used the bike to make local deliveries.

He looked back out into the street at the carnage, which he knew he would never be able to erase from his mind. The store still stank with the stench of the dead. This was his world now. This was his life now.

Then he looked at the rows of packaged and canned goods still on the shelves. He could gather goods and supplies, take the bicycle and head south. He might make it safely; then again, he might not. In the scheme of things, it didn't matter anyway. Trevor felt the grip of his revolver. If he wanted all the pain to stop, he could end it all right now.

"Moment of truth," Trevor said aloud to the empty store.

Living Doll (Carl Hughes)

1

Chazzy found the doll in a dusty, beaten-up suitcase in the attic. She didn't know whether to feel pleased or repelled. In the end she settled for cautious curiosity.

It wasn't a pretty thing. No cherubic lips, cream-smooth complexion or impossibly long eyelashes. This doll had a thin-lipped gash of a mouth, gaunt grey face and eyes as green and cold as winter bracken. Her dress was of grubby gingham, her limbs spindly and strangely elongated like those of Abraham Lincoln: a character that Chazzy had recently learned about at school.

The doll would win no prizes for glamour but something about her, perhaps an air of vulnerability that often clings to the less fortunate, evoked pity in Chazzy's heart. So while crinkling her nose as at an unpleasant smell, the girl also felt strangely protective towards this strange specimen.

'Are you there, Chazelle?' her mother called from the foot of the stairs.

Chazzy bridled. She hated that name. Chazelle sounded like a cross between a cheetah and a gazelle. Melinda Tomlinson, the school bully with a personality as attractive as a warthog's miscarriage, ridiculed her constantly because of *Chazelle* and encouraged her clique of hangers-on to do the same. Chazzy knew it wasn't her name that really got the goat of that crowd, but the fact that she was cleverer

115

than they were, always coming top of the class and that she was Mrs Trickett's favourite.

'Chazelle?' Mum called again.

'Coming.'

Chazzy decided on a whim to keep the doll. Twelve was too old to play with such things but then lots of people older than she collected dolls as a lifelong hobby. In fact Mum still had the teddy bear that she'd been given as a four-year-old. Bruno, he was called, and he sat in tatty splendour on a cushioned chair in Mum and Dad's bedroom.

'What have you got there?' Mum asked when Chazzy stumped down from the attic.

'I found this doll in an old suitcase in the attic.

Mum looked startled for a second, as if glimpsing the Devil's armpits. Then she raised a tenuous smile. 'I haven't seen Lela for twenty years or more,' she said.

'Lela?'

'That's her name. Your gGandma Dorothy gave her to me when I was six or seven. It was the Christmas your grandpa died and it rained non-stop on the day of his funeral. The bus drivers were on strike, I remember, and everything seemed bleak that year.'

'She's a strange-looking thing, isn't she?' Chazzy said, examining the doll judiciously.

'That's what I thought all those years ago. I can't imagine what possessed any toy company to make an object like that and I don't know why my mum gave me anything so peculiar. I suppose Lela must have been cheap and we were going through a hard time just then, what with your grandpa having been off work for so long with the lung complaint that killed him.'

Chazzy's mother was an older facsimile of the girl: fair-haired (although now a touch grey at the roots), face as fresh and guileless as that of an angel, eyes of cornflower blue.

Mother and daughter had been sorting through Grandma Dorothy's things, putting aside the stuff that would have to be thrown out. The old lady's funeral had taken place five days earlier. She'd suffered a stroke two years earlier, then developed cancer, so for the previous eleven months she'd lived with Chazzy's family. Her belongings such as jewellery, old photographs and knick-knacks had been stored in the attic 'ready for the day you're well again and can move back into your own place.' That's what Chazzy's mother had said, though they all knew the day would never arrive.

'It's so long since I've seen Lela that I'd forgotten what a skanky thing she is,' Mum said, taking the doll from Chazzy.

'It isn't her fault.'

'I suppose not. There's a button in her back – you can feel it if you probe about a bit. If you pressed it when Lela was new, she'd say "Hello Mummy", "I'm hungry", or "I'm called Lela". But the voicebox or whatever you call it stopped working when I dunked the doll in a tub of detergent. A stupid thing to do, I know, but at the time I just wanted to give her a bath. My mother rollicked me royally but by then it was too late to put the damage right. I suppose the voice thing must have rusted up or something.'

'Can I have a go?' Chazzy asked.

'If you like, but I warn you it doesn't work any more.'

Chazzy took the doll and, with fixed concentration, she felt with her index finger around Lela's back. She found the button and depressed it but managed to elicit only a farting noise from the doll. It made her laugh.

'You shouldn't laugh at Lela,' Mum said with a severity that Chazzy sensed wasn't altogether make-believe. 'She doesn't like being made fun of. She's sensitive like that.'

'Can I keep her?'

Mum ran a hand through her hair, which had become coated with generations of dust from her mother's belongings. 'If you want to, but Lela's worthless now. I always thought there was something sinister about her. Sometimes she'd talk at night, those three phrases, without me touching the button. It gave me the creeps.'

'I feel sorry for her. She's the kind of doll who always gets neglected when prettier ones are around.'

'*All* dolls are prettier than Lela,' Mum said.

'Ssh. You know what you just told me – she's sensitive.'

Chazzy carried Lela to her bedroom and sat the doll on her dressing table, back resting against the mirror so she seemed to be looking two ways at once. The sunlight of late May filled the room with a cosseting warmth like heated duck-down and the place smelled of Nag Champa incense, which Chazzy liked because it reminded her of that fantastic month she, Mum and Dad spent in India two years back. The walls contained poster pin-ups

118

of hunky pop and movie stars, while a laptop computer stood on a pull-out desk in one corner next to a bookcase housing books by Charles Dickens, George Eliot and Anthony Trollope. Chazzy hadn't opened any of those books, she found the classics boring. They'd been given to her by Grandma Dorothy who felt that all children would become more responsible citizens if only they immersed themselves in nineteenth-century culture. Though Chazzy wouldn't know a Thackeray from a lavatory brush, she had to admit she'd enjoyed the Dickens ghost story, *The Signalman*, that the BBC had screened in its drama schedule last Christmas.

This being the school half-term holiday, Chazzy had no lessons to attend and no homework to be got through so she settled on her bed with *The Hobbit* by J.R.R. Tolkien. Now that was *real* writing. Occasionally she would glance up as if some movement had caught her eye. Each time, she found her attention settling on Lela. The doll's presence unsettled her for a reason she couldn't identify, as if gloom had settled over the bedroom with shadows huddling conspiratorially in corners despite the sunlight. A frown accompanied Chazzy squirreling away her disquiet and returned again and again to Tolkien's fantasy.

After half an hour, unable to concentrate, she left the bedroom where it felt she were escaping from something unhealthy. Something which defied logic. Maybe she should have stuffed the doll back into its suitcase. . Perhaps. But some uneasy inkling told her it was already too late for that.

Dad arrived home from his work at the drawing office looking as if he'd been through a colander. His skin appeared somehow shredded, his hair awry, his usual cheerful self drained away.

'They keep cutting staff and expecting more and more from those of us who're left,' he complained. 'They put us under so much pressure that we're bound to make mistakes, then when we do they say we're sloppy and not doing the jobs we're paid for and aren't going to get a pay rise.'

Where Chazzy and her mother were fair, Dad had reddish hair with natural auburn tints and a face that he said reminded him of a constipated fox.

'My nerves are frazzled,' he said. 'I'm going for a run to get the stress out of my system.'

'Don't be late for tea, Alec,' Mum told him, as she always did before he set off on his thrice-weekly runs.

'Don't worry, I'm only going to St Mark's Church and back. Just about four miles.'

'You'll have to take part in the London Marathon, Dad,' Chazzy said. 'You could raise money for charity.'

'And kill myself in the process. No, I'll never run a marathon but then I only want to stay fit, not win gold for Britain.'

Chazzy watched him go then helped her mother prepare tea. Mum sang softly to herself as if layered with a lightness of spirit.

'Mum, shouldn't we be grieving for Grandma Dorothy?' Chazzy asked.

Her mother stopped singing immediately and looked embarrassed. 'I suppose we should but your grandmother wasn't an easy lady to like, as you well know. She brought me up and did what she considered to be her duty as a mother but I never knew her to have a good word to say about anybody or anything, certainly not about me. And you know better than most that after her stroke she was bitter and twisted, even saying evil things about you and your father. I'm sorry, Chazelle, but I don't miss her.'

Chazzy looked up from the sink. 'I wish you'd stop calling me that.'

'Chazelle? I know you don't like it but it's your name and I think it's pretty.'

'I hate it. When I grow up I'm going to change it to something normal.'

'And you consider *Chazzy* normal, do you?' Her mother smiled, moving from cooker to fridge.

'That isn't what I'll call myself when I get to be eighteen and can change my name legally. I'll settle for Emma or Sarah – even Harper. Something no one'll sneer at anyway.'

'That'll be up to you, but for now you're Chazelle and so you'll remain.'

Chazzy sniffed and didn't answer.

2

Chazzy slept restlessly over that long weekend of the Late Spring Holiday but nothing untoward happened until the small hours of Tuesday morning. It was just before two-thirty when the girl surfaced from a troubled dream, feeling some movement in the bedroom had disturbed her.

She propped herself on one elbow and stared at Lela on the dressing table as had become her

121

unwelcome habit. Moonlight casting a misty radiance into the bedroom, throwing a pale glow around the doll as if she were surrounded by an unhealthy halo. Chazzy realised that if there'd been any movement, it hadn't come from Lela. The doll sat as ever with her back to the mirror, cold green eyes gazing sightlessly into the room.

Suddenly Lela spoke in a creepy, creaky voice full of grinding gears and broken springs, 'I'm hungry.'

Chazzy's heart seemed to skip several beats. Her fingers clenched and unclenched and a quiver ran through her body. She told herself frantically that she ought to feel pleased that Lela had regained her voice after so many years. And maybe that's how she *would* feel, if only she'd pressed the button in the doll's back. As it was, it seemed that in the dead of night Lela had taken on a life that shouldn't be there. Her breath compressed itself in her chest, making Chazzy wish with strange intensity that the doll had remained broken and mute.

Minutes passed as the girl waited in a state of dread for the doll to speak again. Nothing further happened and after a long time, the moon began to wane and Chazzy drifted into an uneasy sleep.

Morning arrived with sunlight laying down a tracery of mosaic diamonds filtered through an abundance of spring leaves. It wasn't yet six o'clock but Chazzy had already risen, moving quietly so as not to disturb her parents. She had something important to do: something she'd resolved to accomplish before breakfast. *Accomplish* was a strange word for it, she knew, but this felt like a task that mightn't be easy to carry out.

In the event, it proved simpler than she'd feared. She grabbed Lela, half expecting to find the doll squirm in her hands, and carried her downstairs and out to the dustbin. Chazzy lifted the lid of the green bin, dropped the doll inside with a sense of relief and returned to her bedroom. Suddenly the incense-scented air felt pure and refreshing, like something newly released from captivity.. Chazzy hugged herself as if she'd completed one of those marathons that Dad had said would be too much for him. She felt she'd got rid of a suffocating menace. She was almost beside herself with joy.

The half-term break over, it was time to return to school. Chazzy attended Broad Pines High, a sprawling redbrick place on the site of a former manor house. It had been in the Pines family from the time of Queen Anne. It was only within the last year or so that girls attending the school had been permitted to wear trousers. The previous head, the crotchety Miss Craddock, had insisted that skirts were de rigueur for all females, even in the worst of winter blizzards. The current head, Mrs Green, being much younger and more trendy, had declared that individuality mustn't be stifled. Unfortunately for Chazzy, Mrs Green interpreted that as meaning, among other things, that all pupils should be allowed to say what they thought, as and when they thought it. Not to the teachers, of course, but to each other.

'Here's little Miss Perfect, our very own arse-crawling goodie – the cringingly named Chazelle.'

That's how Melinda Tomlinson greeted Chazzy as they crossed in the school playground. Melinda's coterie of six hangers-on sniggered and stared at Chazzy as if she were the ugliest creature this side of a slimeball convention.

'Why don't you grow up, Melinda?' Chazzy asked. 'And your friends don't do badly either when it comes to crawling, only it's up *your* arse they're to be found.'

Her black mascara, slash of scarlet lipstick and pointed canines made people think Melinda could have been Dracula's daughter. . Eyes narrowed, glittering, she stepped up to Chazzy so they were almost toe to toe where and she spat green snot into Chazzy's face. Laughing along with her disciples, she turned away and said, 'That's more than you're worth, you little shit. Anyway, I'm having a mega birthday party next week and everybody's invited – everybody except *you*, prissy knickers.'

Chazzy wiped away the snot and saliva with a tissue and feeling the tissue had been tainted irredeemably, she dropped it into a wire waste basket standing close to the staffroom entrance.

Things didn't get better that day. Mrs Trickett picked out Chazzy's essay on the Roman empire as a first-class piece of writing and told the other pupils that this was the standard they should aspire to. Instead of pleasing Chazzy, it embarrassed her acutely as she felt the glaring hatred of Melinda and her cohorts burning into her back. The envy of others in the class didn't help, either.

At the end of afternoon lessons, Melinda came up behind Chazzy and snatched her satchel. She then tipped its contents over the playground and trampled them underfoot, laughing at Chazzy's dismay.

'If you think you're so hard done by, teacher's pet, why don't you try to stop me?' Melinda asked.

Chazzy knew she'd be in for a severe beating if she got into a fight with Melinda, a girl not only several inches taller than she but who looked as if her skeleton were composed of iron girders and who had legs made to support verandas. Besides, Mum and Dad had always impressed on her the notion that bullies weren't to be indulged when they picked on those physically weaker than themselves. 'Stand up to them with dignity, not with fists when you know you'll get the crap knocked out of you.' That's what Dad had told her.

Chazzy wasn't sure that this advice always held good, as Mr Platton the vicar preached that all bullies were cowards at heart and would back down if you met violence with violence. That didn't seem to Chazzy to be a very Christian way of thinking (turn the other cheek and all that), and anyway she wasn't willing to put the reverend's bit of homespun philosophy to the test. After all, Mr Platton had probably never had to trade blows with somebody who displayed the finesse of a pissed-off Sherman tank. So Chazzy picked up her broken and soiled things, packed them into her satchel and made her way home.

It would be easy for her to mess up her schoolwork in future, to draw Mrs Trickett's wrath rather than her praise, but that would be playing into the sulphurous hands of Melinda and her toadies. Besides, Mum and Dad were proud of their smart daughter and Chazzy wasn't going to disappoint them for the likes of any braggart with big tits, as Melinda had.

She could of course complain to Mrs Green the headteacher, asking her to prevent further bullying; but that wasn't an option. Janice Longfellow had got her parents to confront the head about that very thing after months of torment at the hands of Melinda, and Mrs Green had put the bullying down to *banter and playfulness* and told Janice not to be so sensitive. In other words, to get a life. Which had delighted Melinda and since then her persecution of Janice had intensified. Now Janice had started self-harming, cutting herself with razor blades, and Mrs Green's only advice to the parents was to take the girl to see a psychotherapist.

The day had been every bit as grotty as Chazzy had feared it would be and the grottiness wasn't over yet.

When she reached home, she found her Mum had finished her shift at the hospital, where she was a sister in the acute unit, but was suffering from a blinding migraine. She'd gone to bed after dosing herself with a drug that never seemed to work and she had left a note asking Chazzy to be a good girl and see to tea for herself and her father.

Chazzy didn't mind cooking; in fact she enjoyed it although Mum had convinced herself that being a vegetarian, Chazzy would eventually turn into a turnip or something.

Before preparing tea, Chazzy went upstairs to get changed out of her school things and into a yellow sweatshirt and maroon jeans. And that's

126

when the afternoon descended from the miserable to the sinister.

She found Lela sitting on the dressing table again, her back against the mirror and staring with green-eyed vacuity into the room. The doll was splay-legged, stretchy-armed and seemed to Chazzy to be exuding a menace that ought never have been released from that tatty suitcase in the attic.

From the door, where she'd come up as short as if meeting a tram going the other way, Chazzy sidled into the room, her gaze fixed on the doll. She wouldn't have been surprised to see Lela get up and totter across the top of the dressing table.

'What're you doing back here?' the girl whispered. A rhetorical question, for dolls couldn't talk. Or at least, most of them couldn't.

The answer, when it occurred to her, seemed obvious. Mum must have found Lela in the dustbin and for some reason, a really inexplicable one, she'd restored the doll to Chazzy's dressing table.

Chazzy's instinct was to dump Lela in the bin again but she told herself that would be tantamount to saying Mum should mind her own business. The reality, and there really was a twist to her logic, was that she dreaded the thought of touching the doll again. She feared that if she returned Lela to the bin, the wretched doll might find her way back to the bedroom once more without the aid of human hands. At a churning subconscious level, where the darkest dreams and nightmares dwelt, Chazzy didn't want to risk or even consider that possibility.

This day really had turned out like the business end of smallpox.

3

Cloud built during the evening and when Chazzy turned in for the night she found that dense drizzle had begun to fall beyond the bedroom window like celestial dandruff. It was a cheerless sight and one that matched her mood. She had a foreboding of more than natural night-time darkness emerging during the coming hours.

And she was right.

The red numerals on the bedside clock were showing two thirty-three when Chazzy surfaced with a jolt from a sleep punctuated by rags of restless dreams. Something had disturbed her: some movement that had no place in her bedroom in the dead of night.

The drizzle had turned to steady rain, pattering against the windowpane like a million centipedes in clogs. It wasn't this sound, the work of nature, that had aroused Chazzy. She didn't mind rain. Or wind or even lightning. No, the dread that thumped in her heart now concerned Lela: the thing she'd come to hate and fear. For she believed that's what had wrenched her from sleep.

Too scared to move, hoping she'd simply been spooked by a forgotten dream, she lay for a minute. Two minutes.

Then the doll spoke. In the same creepy, creaky voice as before, but this time uttering something that shouldn't have been possible, Lela said, 'Daddy's going to die.' The broken springs and grinding gears were mechanical things but somehow they managed to convey not just menace

128

but also a sense of glee as if the doll had become more than the sum of her machine-driven parts.

Chazzy was petrified. She squirmed up the mattress until she was sitting upright, her knees humped beneath the duvet. Her trembling hand reached out and turned on the bedside light, then squinched her eyes in its sudden brightness. She stifled a scream. The doll, instead of sitting on the dressing table, was perched on the side of the bed less than an arm's length from where the girl had been sleeping.

The doll's gash of a mouth, cold green eyes and gaunt grey face seemed in some indefinable way to hint at mockery, at a wickedness no toy should possess. The spindly, elongated arms dangled like tentacles that on a whim could wrap themselves around a child's throat.

Sobbing, Chazzy snatched the doll and flung her away. Lela hit the wall with a soft thud, like wet rags and fell in a heap by the door.

'What d'you want with me?' Chazzy whispered. 'Why don't you leave me alone? And you aren't meant to say anything except what Mum told me you could say.'

The doll, being a mere toy, didn't answer. Nor did Lela speak again that night although Chazzy remained awake, with the light on, in tense expectation of more witchery.

4

Morning arrived with thick mist and grey rain more suited to November than the start of summer. Chazzy made her way to school wearing a crinkly

129

blue anorak that had been bought from an outdoor centre at Llanberis in Snowdonia during a family holiday the previous autumn. The wild mountain air and freedom from care seemed so far away now that desolation cloaked the girl like an icy mantle. Cars, lorries and buses were throwing up muddy globules on this filthy morning, tyres hissing on the greasy roads like angry serpents that had been trodden on.

Chazzy felt confused and raddled. Should she have told Mum about the impossibility of what had happened during the night? Mum would never believe the doll capable of uttering anything other than the three phrases the thing had been programmed to spew out. She'd say Chazzy had been dreaming and no one could blame her for that. After all, dolls didn't come to life. Only, in this case, Lela had.

The morning lessons passed in a fuzz of inattention that caused Mrs Trickett to speak more sharply to Chazzy than she'd ever done before. Chazzy scarcely heard what the teacher said; hardly even registered the sniggers of Melinda Tomlinson and the usual suspects who cosied up to her. Melinda was in a particularly bitchy mood that morning. Before lessons began, she'd been boasting of her coming birthday party and dictating to her cronies the sort of expensive presents she expected them to deliver.

At lunchtime, instead of drifting off to the school canteen, Chazzy sat in the empty classroom pondering the implausibilities of what she'd experienced. Perhaps it really had been no more than a dream. But no, seductive though that argument was, it didn't stand up to scrutiny. This morning, the cursed doll had remained where Chazzy had flung her in the early hours. That was a fact, not a dream. And the words Lela had uttered: they'd been robotic in a cranky way but they were clear enough, not to be confused with 'I'm called Lela', 'Hello Mummy', or 'I'm hungry'. Yet logic, and Chazelle prided herself on being blessed with a fair dose of it, suggested that this particular conundrum went beyond the range of implausibility and entered the territory of impossibility.

So the lunch hour passed and the kids returned to class for the first of two periods of English. This was a subject in which Chazzy normally excelled but now she had to endure more reproaches from Mrs Trickett.

'Pull yourself together, girl,' Mrs Trickett scolded. She was a spindly, bespectacled woman with a stick-like nose, she resembled most people's idea of the archetypal spinster. Indeed, Melanie Tomlinson spread it about on what she termed 'the best authority' that Mrs Trickett had never allowed the unfortunate Mr Trickett to get into her knickers.

It was midway through the second period that the classroom door opened and Mrs Green, the headteacher, entered. Chazzy frowned as the head tiptoed across to the teacher's desk as if treading through something from the rear end of a giraffe. Mrs Green usually left the teachers to get on with their work without imposing herself on them outside the staffroom. Now as she and Mrs Trickett went into a huddle, an expectant hush fell over the twenty-three pupils sitting behind their desks.

Icy fingers ran up and down Chazzy's spine, freezing her marrow, as the eyes of the two women picked her out with what could only be described as expressions of mega tragedy.

'Chazelle, will you come with me and Mrs Trickett, please?' Mrs Green said. 'The rest of you, get on with your work and if I hear a sound from this classroom there'll be trouble.'

Chazzy knew without needing to have it broadcast in deafening decibels what this was all about.

In the corridor, Mrs Green took her hand and Mrs Trickett put a consoling arm around her shoulder.

'Now then, Chazelle, I want you to prepare yourself for a shock,' Mrs Green said. 'Your mother's in my office. She'll explain things that are far better coming from her than from me.'

As they made their way to the head's office, Chazzy found a baneful mantra running through her mind. *The doll. Lela. The doll. Lela.*

She found her mother in tears. Sobbing, in fact, with a damp handkerchief clutched in her hand. She looked ancient, haggard, as worn as a statue ruined by acid rain.

'My secretary's fetching a pot of tea,' Mrs Green said in sepulchral tones. 'And of course Mrs Trickett and I are here for you both. We'll do whatever we can.'

Mum had been sitting on the visitors' side of Mrs Green's desk but now she stood up, staggered forward and hugged Chazzy.

'Dad's dead isn't he?' Chazzy said. She felt she were suffocating yet at the same time experiencing a strange calmness, as if an inevitability had been released at last.

132

Mum nodded, sniffing, nose oozing greasy snot. 'It was a heart attack. At work. He'd been under incredible pressure to do more and more – I'm sure that's what caused it. He tried to keep fit but the body can stand only so much stress.'

'Mum, you won't believe this but I knew it was going to happen,' Chazzy said.

'Don't be silly. How could you?'

'Lela told me. During the night – she said "Daddy's going to die."'

Mum hugged her tighter. 'You had a nasty dream, that's all. None of us could possibly know this would happen.'

Which was pretty much what Chazzy had expected her to say.

Rain lashed the window, washing down in cascades. Chazzy felt her own heart were flooded too, with dread and anger. She wanted to scream, to yell, to rage at the malevolence that had entered their lives.

Instead she buried her face in her mother's shoulder and wept.

5

Chazzy and her mother slept little that night and neither of them went to bed. Chazzy dozed on the sofa and her mother in one of the squashy armchairs that she and Alec had bought in a sale at Price's bargain-basement furniture shop so long ago. She choked up now, perhaps recalling how proud they'd been on saving enough money to replace the old suite they'd been given as a wedding present by Alec's parents.

133

Mother and daughter were joined that harrowing night by Alec's distraught widowed mother, Trudy, who occupied the other armchair. Chazzy thought that Grandma Trudy, by far the favourite of her two grandmothers, probably didn't sleep a wink. At any rate the elderly lady was awake and grieving silently every time Chazzy surfaced from her brief dozes.

If Chazzy hadn't been so distressed herself, she would have attempted to comfort Grandma Trudy. In good times the pair had spent hours together, Chazzy enjoying her grandmother's fabulous tales of pixies, elves, pirates and ghosts. Grandma Trudy always had a treasury of such stories and she and Chazzy doted on each other. Ramrod-straight, brisk, belying her sixty-odd years, Grandma Trudy loved high-octane thrills and anything that gave her an adrenaline rush. Even at this harrowing time she epitomised stolidity but Chazzy sensed the wretchedness enveloping her heart.

Morning seeped in at last. A dismal morning it was, thoroughly matching the mood of Chazzy and the two adults. Lowering cloud, as heavy as a diseased bladder, hung over the town, blowing dingy drizzle on a callous wind.

'Go and change into fresh things, Chazelle, while your grandma and I get breakfast ready,' Mum said when it became obvious that none of them would manage any more sleep.

Chazzy was still wearing her school uniform. Her blouse and trousers had become crumpled and creased and she felt as if ladlesful of sweat coated her body. She stumped upstairs obediently and washed herself in the bathroom before, with

134

monumental reluctance, entering her bedroom where the doll remained in a heap by the door. Chazzy avoided glancing at the loathsome object.

Determined to spend no longer in the bedroom than necessity dictated, she dragged a pair of blue jeans from her wardrobe and was just plucking a turquoise sweatshirt from a drawer in the dressing table when the thing happened that she'd dreaded.

The doll spoke.

Chazzy knew it was about to happen even before the words emerged. A chirring, rasping sound emerged from the bundle by the door, then Lela said with a distinctness that belied her broken springs and rusted gears, 'Grandma Trudy's going to die.'

Chazzy leapt back dropping the fresh clothes and reacting as if stung by a near-lethal dose of electricity, screamed, '*No, you bastard! Shut the fuck up and leave us alone!*'

Sobbing, feeling she were coming apart in scorching fragments, she bolted from the room. As she did so she heard the doll emit an oleaginous, creaky laugh.

Less than a minute later, bawling and blubbing like a toddler who'd witnessed horrors beyond comprehension, Chazzy erupted into the kitchen. Her mother and grandmother turned, as startled as if the roof had fallen in.

'Good God, Chazelle, whatever's the matter?' Mum asked, almost dropping the kettle.

'It's that voodoo doll, Lela,' Chazzy yelled. 'She says Grandma Trudy's going to die.'

Mum and Grandma Trudy exchanged alarmed glances as Chazzy hugged them both, drawing them into a tight embrace.

'The poor girl's hysterical with grief,' Grandma Trudy said, as distressed as if she'd experienced the horror herself.

'No I'm not,' Chazzy insisted, her throat choked with snot and saliva. 'The doll talks to me when I'm on my own and she says terrible things. She told me Dad was going to die and now she says you are too, Grandma.'

'Calm down, Chazelle – your grandma isn't going to die,' Mum said.

'Of course I'm not,' Grandma Trudy declared. 'I'm as healthy and strong as an ox. We're all upset about your dad, Chazzy, that's to be expected. Imagination's a fine thing when it creates magic but sometimes, at times of sorrow like this, it can conjure nasty thoughts and illusions.'

'But I tell you Lela really talks – she's cursed.' Chazzy stamped her foot and realised how foolish and immature that must seem coming from a twelve-year-old girl. She didn't want to appear childish, not at her age; she wanted only to convince Mum and Grandma Trudy that what she'd experienced was real, not the ravings of a lunatic with crazily firing synapses in the brain.

'You'll feel better after you've had some breakfast,' Mum said, which infuriated Chazzy so much that she felt like hitting out at anyone and anything within reach.

Chazzy clenched her fists, holding herself rigid with tension but determined to appear calm and rational, she said, 'You've got to believe me. Lela's haunted or cursed or something and she's evil.'

'Please, Chazelle . . .' Mum began.

'And don't call me that!' Chazzy yelled.

'I'm sorry, pet. I know you like being called Chazzy and I'll try to remember. But you must see we're all upset and you're only making things worse for me and your grandma as well as for yourself. Of course you were close to your dad and he adored you, but this talk of a haunted doll is just foolish. Surely you understand that?'

Beyond the kitchen window, sycamores shivered and pampas grass bent almost double in a strengthening wind that rumbled around the house like a beast striving to find a way in. It was a bleak scene but compared to the iciness in Chazzy's heart it could have been the very apotheosis of summer.

Chazzy realised nothing she said would convince Mum or Grandma Trudy of the truth and she collapsed inwardly. It was as if a great stultifying weariness and defeat had settled on her, draining her strength and gobbling her willpower like a bug-eyed leviathan that fed on human emotion.

Little was said after that. The three ate breakfast in near silence, grief and confusion creating an awkward distance between them. Chazzy scarcely noticed the scrambled egg, the toast and marmalade that Mum served up. She didn't even think much about Lela. It was as if unawareness as dense as sodden cotton wool now filled her skull.

'I'd better go home and change into fresh clothes,' Grandma Trudy said at last, carrying her

137

plate from the breakfast bar. 'But we need to be together so I'll come straight back. That is, if dear old Gertie'll start up. She's on her last legs, I think.' Gertie was her ancient Ford Fiesta, a rattletrap of a vehicle that burned almost as much oil as petrol and frequently broke down in the most ill-chosen places and usually in the direst weather. In happier times, Grandma Trudy joked that she had a hotline to both the AA and RAC and was on first-name terms with the personnel of both those motoring organisations.

Chazzy continued to sit at the breakfast bar, staring blankly at the mottled Formica top. At the periphery of consciousness she knew Mum and Grandma Trudy were worrying about her, which raised guilt in her heart as she knew they already had far too much to care about without her adding to their woes. But still she sat as Grandma Trudy and Mum left the kitchen. A minute or two later she heard Gertie's engine grumping to itself, the starter motor and battery struggling to elicit a response from the car's innards. Eventually the engine fired, chugging and chuntering, and Grandma Trudy set off.

On returning to the kitchen, Mum said, 'You're still in your school uniform, Chazelle. Sorry, I mean Chazzy. You'd better get changed so you'll be fresh when your grandmother gets back.'

'I won't go into the bedroom on my own,' Chazzy said. 'Not while Lela's there.'

'That wretched doll has a lot to answer for. You've fixated on something unhealthy. Never mind, we'll go upstairs together.'

Even then it required all of Chazzy's resolution to follow her mother upstairs.

And it didn't surprise her to find that Lela had now returned to the dressing table, all gangly legs and arms, sitting with her back to the mirror, staring with cold indifference into a room that had become polluted by her presence.

When she was through changing her clothes, Chazzy went downstairs with her mother and together they wept for Dad and, in Chazzy's case, for what she feared was about to happen next.

And it did.

When Grandma Trudy failed to return after two hours, Mum began to grow worried. A third hour passed and she phoned Trudy's house. The ring tone went on and on. No answer.

'Perhaps she's on her way back,' Mum said with a degree of tension that spoke of an ugly foreboding.

It was just after one o'clock when a police car pulled up at the door. Chazzy, standing at the window, knew what was about to happen. Not the details, just the essence of what was to enfold in the next few minutes. She felt hollow, as if a great cosmic purgative had scoured her insides.

Two police officers entered the house: a man with a cherry nose and a woman with kind eyes and a frizz of hair wisping from beneath her hat.

Gertie's engine had blown up in Dove Street, the main thoroughfare through town and the car had come to a grinding stop. A tailgating lorry travelling behind, far too close for safety, ploughed into the back of the vehicle.

Grandma Trudy hadn't stood a chance.

6

Relatives and friends called at the house, all full of condolences and exclamations of disbelief about tragedy having struck twice in successive days. When Chazzy tried to tell them that evil had been visited on the family in the form of a deformed doll, they tutted and sympathised with her mother, saying they realised what a shocking psychological impact these deaths must be having on the girl.

Even after what had happened, Chazzy's mother refused to countenance the idea that a doll could be imbued with malevolence. The capacity to produce monstrous events wasn't in the gift of an inanimate toy, she insisted. Chazzy had been overwrought and only imagined the talking doll. As for the rest, coincidences happened all the time and Trudy ought never to have trusted in that blasted car: a death trap if ever there'd been one.

Chazzy escaped from all the tears, the condolences and the hushed words of solace and reminiscence. Resolute, enraged rather than fearful, she went to her bedroom, snatched the doll with a hatred previously alien to her nature and in a demonic fury ripped off its head and limbs. As she did so, the doll spoke again, possibly for the last time. That same grating, rusting rasp. The thing said, 'You'll be sorry.'

'Bollocks to that and fuck you,' Chazzy responded. She meant to ensure that never again could the doll spread its malignant tentacles into the life of her family.

Unseen by friends and relations, who were too preoccupied by their own concerns to wonder what she was doing, she carried the doll in its various

140

pieces out to the garden where Dad used to burn rubbish in a brazier. Chazzy dumped Lela's remains in there, fetched some paraffin from the shed, soaked the doll in the stuff and set it alight.

The thing burned with a putrid odour like rotten eggs. The flames were purple and blue, immolating the plastic and fake hair and gingham, reducing it all to ashes.

'May you rot in a snake pit of your own wickedness,' Chazzy said. 'Now go to Hell.'

She knew that Mrs Penton, the neighbourhood gossip who lived next door, was watching this through her kitchen window. Mrs Penton never missed anything that happened in the avenue and was given to putting her own malicious spin on even the most innocuous things. God knew what she'd make of this. Chazzy didn't give a tuppeny damn. Mrs Penton could go to the devil in a horse-drawn hearse for all she cared.

There was no sense of triumph in Chazzy's step or her bearing as she returned to the mournful gathering in the house. Too much tragedy had been wrought for even a grain of satisfaction to prevail.

Mum was telling Auntie Eileen and Uncle Bob that there'd be a joint funeral for Alec and Trudy. Mother and son would be laid to rest together in Mount Pleasant Burial Ground: one of those modern cemeteries with lots of trees and acres of grass where the dead lay below stone plaques set into the manicured lawns. No monumental weeping angels or granite headstones or lichen-stained crosses there. Mount Pleasant was a memory storehouse of lives well lived, a place of reflection, rather than a dismal and morbid wasteland of mourning.

The relatives and friends finally dispersed, leaving Chazzy alone with her mother. Chazzy felt washed out, grainy-eyed from weeping, defeated. The jinx doll had gone but the thing had left immeasurable sorrow as its legacy. Dad and Grandma Trudy, two of the lights of Chazzy's life, the people she revered and whose words she had accepted as gospel, were gone beyond recall and she blamed herself. If only she'd never discovered that hideous thing in the attic, both Dad and Grandma Trudy would still be alive, the family would be intact and there'd be no blight to confront for years to come. And Chazzy was under no illusion: that blight really would last for years. In fact she doubted she'd ever cease to condemn herself for the cataclysm she'd unleashed. As for Mum, she had been robbed of the man to whom she'd been devoted and with whom she had expected to remain happily united for another forty years or more.

The long summer day dwindled to a late twilight, the mantle of night not falling until after ten o'clock. It was nearer eleven when Chazzy and Mum surrendered to exhaustion and made their way to bed.

'Wrecked though I am, I doubt I'll get any sleep,' Mum said.

'I'm sorry, Mum – I truly am,' Chazzy said.

Her mother probably thought she was merely sympathising for the coming insomnia, but that wasn't what Chazzy had meant.

Mother and daughter parted on the landing, to go to their respective bedrooms.

Chazzy opened the door of her room, turned on the light . . . and found Lela sitting on the dressing

142

table. The doll's gash of mouth seemed to be smirking as if in mockery of Chazzy, or perhaps in gloating glee at Lela's own indestructibility.

Girl and doll spent what seemed like aeons staring at each other. Chazzy didn't feel scared, merely defeated. Weary of a battle lost.

She backed out on to the landing, muscles and sinews weighed as if with sacks of lead. She went to her mother's bedroom and said, 'Mum, can I sleep in here with you tonight?'

Mum's look of sympathy struck like a stiletto to Chazzy's heart. 'Of course you can, Chazzy. I can understand you not wanting to be on your own.'

I wouldn't be on my own – that's the trouble, Chazzy thought.

Outside, a cold wind like something out of December, buffeted the window as if a malign entity were trying to gain entry.

7

Some of Chazzy's classmates expressed sympathy and strove to be kind to her, but the majority refrained from saying anything. They were too afraid of reprisals from Melinda Tomlinson. That girl, the school bully, spoke to Chazzy only once. She said, 'It's a pity it wasn't you that croaked, you little shit. And if you expect me to invite you to my party tomorrow because I feel sorry for you, there's more chance of Ma Trickett handing out dildos to give us all a thrill.'

Chazzy had called at Murrell's newsagent's shop on her way to school to buy a birthday card for Melinda. She also had a special gift for her tormentor wrapped in her satchel and ready for delivery.

Feigning a migraine, Chazzy skipped the last lesson of the day. She left the school and threaded her way through Torrington Terrace and Bury Drive, places in the best end of town, and reached number nineteen Broad View just after three o'clock. This was Melinda's home. It was a strange place: something that looked like a bungalow that decided to become a house, then changed its mind halfway through.

Chazzy left the unsigned card and the gift on Melinda's doorstep. She didn't know what Melinda's reaction would be on opening the gaily-wrapped package and finding inside it a weird doll with a thin-lipped gash of mouth, gaunt grey face and eyes as green and cold as winter bracken. No, Chazzy didn't know what the reaction would be but she could guess. Melinda would probably express disgust and chuck the repulsive thing in her dustbin. Only, she might find she couldn't get rid of Lela so easily.

Satisfied but strangely lacking any sense of triumph, Chazzy made her way home.

'You're a bit early,' Mum said.

'I had a headache so Mrs Trickett told me to come home,' Chazzy replied.

'How are you now? You shouldn't have gone to school today, not while you're so upset for your dad and grandma.'

'I'm fine. Really. I think I'll go upstairs and get my homework done.'

The house seemed unnaturally still, as if bricks, mortar and plaster could collectively embody lungs and heartbeats. Only this house now had no heart.

Chazzy was about to open her bedroom door when a presentiment of something unhealthy awaiting her on the other side descended like dust from the ceiling. Like that dust in the attic where the tatty suitcase still lay.

Was it movement she heard from the bedroom? Movement or mere imagination?

Her hand had been hovering on the handle of the door. Now it fell to her side.

She turned away, feeling like a helpless and lost little girl as she called downstairs, 'Hello Mummy – I'm hungry.'

A Woman Sporned (Diane Arrelle)

Sweat beading on her forehead, Andi reached up and pushed the gray streaked hair off her face. *This heat's so oppressive*, she thought and decided to drive into town later to buy an electric fan. In the meantime, she wiped at the sweat with her forearm smearing it into her eyes. "Shit," she muttered and blinked to ease the burning sensation, then got down on her knees and examined the ancient indoor-outdoor carpeting covering the foundation of the screened-in sunroom.

The earthy smell of mildew hit her like a physical blow.

"Ugh!" She recoiled and blinked her eyes harder. "Can't put this off any longer," she told herself and picked up the scissors from the floor next to her. Feeling tension release from inside her she started hacking at the cheap carpeting like a slasher in a B movie. As the slit grew with ragged edges of rotting fabric, she grabbed the edges and ripped, revealing the concrete floor underneath. She tore violently, grunting with the effort and driven by a need to do something constructive to fill her time. She finally stopped when the entire center of the floor was exposed.

"Just my luck," Andi snorted, staring at the cracked, crumbling foundation. The musty smell grew, filling the entire area with an awful, stale stench that made her wince and breathe through her mouth. She gaped dumbly at the cracks that ran down the middle of the floor from house doorway to screened doorway. There were fat, black, spongy bumps about an inch high pushing up through the tiny pieces of broken concrete.

"Gross!" She grunted and retreated into the tiny cabin buried in the New Jersey Pine Barrens. Wishing for a drink, a real drink, just to get the smell from her nose, she sniffed and swore the scent had followed her inside.

She sat on the old sofa and studied her new home. It was a sweet tiny, cedar shake, one-story house at the end of a dirt road and Andi realized that even with the rotting floor in the sunroom and the air conditioner out of commission, she was still incredibly lucky. She'd only been casually friendly with Janine through Alcoholics' Anonymous and now Janine had given her this house.

And what better time than now, when she'd lost her job and couldn't pay the rent on her apartment. Andi smiled at her new home, got up and sprayed air freshener, then mixed herself an iced tea. Moving to the rocking chair on the front pouch she decided to take in the sounds of nature. The squirrels chittered while jumping from tree to tree and the birds called out in their myriad voices. She sighed, closed her eyes and listened.

Five minutes later, bored with nature, she let her mind wander to other things. She opened her eyes and muttered, "I wonder what happened to Janine?" She stopped a moment, enjoying the companionable the sound of her voice over the sounds of the pine forest. "I wish I could thank her. I wish I knew why she gave up a great place like this. And I wish I knew why me. Why's she leave it to me?"

147

She had been at her wits end, packing to move and no place to go when the letter arrived just three days ago. It had been brief.

It read: <u>Andi, I know you will love it here and I won't be needing my house anymore. It's yours. Pick up the keys and the deed at my lawyer's office.</u>

Andi, had glanced at the eviction notice posted on her apartment door and didn't stop to think or wonder or anything. She just thanked the fates, loaded her car with her few belongings and drove from the coal filled mountains of Scranton, Pennsylvania to the totally flat, seemingly endless pinelands of southern New Jersey.

"So odd," Andi said for about the hundredth time since arriving. "So perfect too." She finished with both her tea and her failed attempt at communing with nature and went back to the screened-in room at the rear of the cabin. She sprayed more air freshener, although the room was completely opened to the outside air, and then she finished ripping the fake carpet away from the edges where it has been glued down.

She stood surveying her handiwork.

And gasped.

The black bumps had grown in what had to be some sort of record time. They seemed to be reaching up, struggling to break free from the broken floor. The big, fat, fingerlike growths, now several inches tall, looked like the appendages of the Elephant Man if he had had fifteen hands.

Andi shuddered, felt goose bumps crawling up her arms. She edged away, backing into her living room and locked the sunroom door. She couldn't stop shivering in the oppressive indoor heat. The

148

growths had to be more than nature at its ugliest. She just knew that they had to be something supernatural, something evil. That smell from hell, that rapid growth. They definitely couldn't be natural at all. She ran outside into the driveway and stood, confusion and fear blurring her thoughts.

After a few minutes of standing in the shade of the tall, skinny pines, smelling the incredible, calming, evergreen scent of the Barrens, Andi felt her heart rate return to normal and she snorted in annoyance at herself. "Get a grip girl. Show some spine, so you got something nasty growing out back, so it looks like the hands of a yeti. I don't understand what is going on, but this is my house now, all mine, and no matter what's happening back there, I'm gonna find out about it and I'm going to make it go away."

Squaring her shoulders with an exaggerated motion, Andi went back out to the sunroom. She shuddered and gagged, bile burning her throat. The things were even bigger and more defined. She took pictures of them with her phone, then grabbing her purse, she drove to the nearby little town. She checked into a cheap motel that looked like it had originally been chicken coops in the 1950s and charged the room to a card already close to being maxed out. She then walked over to the local hardware and feed store.

The electric fans were whirring, their bright red price tags spinning in their wind and Andi realized she couldn't afford any of the prices. She glanced over to the leathery old man behind the counter and said, "Hi, I'm Andi, I just moved into the cabin at the end of Shawtowne Road. Stupid me, I smelled something bad in the sunroom and ripped up the carpet and to my utter surprise I found these."

She showed the photos to the clerk and asked, "Ever see anything like this before?"

He studied the screen for a few seconds then grinned. "Dead man's fingers!"

"Andi frowned, "You're joking, right?"

The clerk called to a guy in jeans and a long-sleeve, plaid shirt standing a few feet away, "Yo, George, what do you think this is?"

Andi was almost more fascinated that he was wearing a long sleeve shirt and work jeans in this weather than his answer. "Henry, you know them's dead man's fingers! Why you wastin' my time."

"Little lady wanted to know."

She looked from man to man wondering if they were fooling around with the out-of-towner. "What are dead man's fingers anyway. They just grew in a matter of minutes."

"Fungus." Henry answered.

"Fungus?" Andi repeated.

"Yep, mushrooms." George added rubbing his callous hands together. "Yep, we got a wide variety of fungi better known as mushrooms growing in the barrens. Give the area a couple of damp, humid days and they'll all come out to visit us. Totally harmless, you know, as long as you don't eat 'em, or smoke 'em."

Andi gave a self depreciating smile, "Not to worry, not my vice of choice."

Henry held up a slim, paperback book about the local pinelands. "This book will fill you in just fine, little lady. Whole chapter on the fungi."

150

Hating to do it, but feeling obligated, Andi took seven dollars from her wallet, gingerly fingered the few twenties left, and purchased the book. She sat on a flat of grain sacks and opened it to the chapter they'd just discussed. Looking at the images in front of her, she laughed, embarrassed and feeling foolish. "Dead Man's Fingers! Quite the appropriate name isn't it."

Out of the corner of her eyes she saw, Henry hand a bottle to George who took a sip and handed it back. "Oops sorry, ma'am. Local wine. Care for a sip."

Every fiber within her screamed no, but Andi decided that she could handle one sip, and she certainly didn't want to appear rude to these two locals.

Taking the bottle, she tried to hide the trembling of her hands as she tilted it and took a drink, a big one. She'd only intended a small sip, but temptation won out. Anyway, it was good wine. "Thanks," she said, regretfully handing it back. She'd been clean and sober for almost half a year and knew that she'd just made a mistake.

Henry smiled with pride, "My vineyard. Here take a full bottle, a welcome to our town gift. Share it with your friends."

She took the sealed bottle and thanked the men, then headed back to the motel for the night. She stared at the bottle for hours while the TV blared in the background. Share it with friends, he had said. Well, she didn't have any friends. People like her never had friends, people like her were meant to live alone, to be alone. That was why she drank, to keep the loneliness away.

151

"Not this time!" she snapped and went to bed. Tossing and thrashing, Andi was plagued by dreams of strange, silent men with dead hands who were hiding in the forest around her new home. She woke, sweat soaked although the window air conditioner unit churned out chilled air, and thought about Janine. A loner, a loser like herself, they'd been AA friends. Janine, the only person she'd had any emotional connection with in years. Janine, her person of choice to fall off the wagon with. She thought about their deep, drunken discussions involving loneliness and futility. Discussions about how their dreams had all shriveled and died, about the husbands, the kids, the fulfillment that had evaded them both. *What had happened to Janine*, she wondered. *Was she dead? Commit suicide?*

Andi now owned the house of a probable dead woman. Too creepy, yet it was the only thing in this world she owned besides her ten-year-old car. The urge to run away was so strong she had to force herself to stay in bed. Turn away from the house and she'd have to live in that car. Not much of a choice at all, she decided and drifted off to more bad dreams.

Early the next morning Andi drove back home, feeling sheepish and yet apprehensive. She parked and went around to the back of the place and looked through the slightly rusted screens. The black fingers had shriveled overnight. They sagged to the ground becoming deflated looking black smears on the floor.

"Oooh even grosser!"

She cleaned up the wilted fungus and then washed the unbroken parts of the floor hoping to get all the last traces. She stopped for lunch and thumbed through the chapter on mushrooms again. "Amazing! Who have thought there could be so many varieties of toadstools," she said realizing most didn't resemble toadstools at all, but rather malignant tumor-like growths clinging to the sides of mossy rocks and pushing out from under decaying brush.

She spent the afternoon sipping iced tea, wishing it were something stronger, but knowing she should never go that route ever again. She tried to forget about the wine bottle in the car as well as the sunroom with the cracked floor and musty smell, but they both just kept nagging away at her. "Maybe I'll tear it down. I could plant a garden of flowers in it's place. Nice soil, the smell of roses and gladiolas would drown out the smell of mold forever."

She got up and rushed to the shed to see if she had any tools that would smash the concrete foundation to pebbles. Excitement bubbled through her as she searched the dark, dank interior. At last, she had something to do, something to occupy her empty hours, something to take her mind off drinking and how much she missed it.

Suddenly she saw it, a sledge hammer. She couldn't lift it, so she dragged it out in a two handed grip, carefully walking backwards. She had no idea what she was going to do with a tool that was so heavy she couldn't lift it, but felt sure she'd figure it out.

Back inside the sunroom, she stopped short. Her lips curled down and her nose crinkled up. The smell almost knocked her over. She stared at the new growths standing erect and tall and although she was fighting fear and revulsion, laughter suddenly exploded out of her. She couldn't take her eyes off the newest mushrooms to grace her home. Deep pink, they all looked exactly like penises.

"I have a penis garden growing through the floor of my house!"

She laughed so hard, her knees gave out and she sank onto the clammy floor. "My god, I've got body parts taking over my home!" she giggled. "What next? No wait, I don't want to know!"

She jumped up and the godawful smell followed her into the kitchen. She sprayed the can of freshener until it was empty and then sat to read her book on fungus again. She thought her phallic mushrooms would have a cool, creepy name just like the black fingers, but there were no genitalia names listed for them. All she found was that they were a variety of stinkhorn mushrooms, and lord, did they stink. She sighed and decided to drive into town again, get away from that smell and pick up something for dinner.

Pushing the shopping cart around the small grocery store helped her feel normal. By the time she'd finished, she was ready to face the onslaught that nature was apparently throwing at her. She went back to the hardware store to see if Henry was there. She was feeling lonely and his being old and scarecrow-like, didn't deter her. She thought that perhaps the mushrooms had made her feel so strangely horny.

"Hey, Henry, remember me?" she said, "I just inherited Janine Trainer's house. Any tales about the place or the area? Folk lore?"

The man rubbed his chin a moment then brightened. "Every inch of the Barrens has some lore attached to it. This town was once five miles that way," he said pointing in the direction Andi now resided. "But it moved after a terrible forest fire. Everything was destroyed, but that was more than a hundred years ago. Some say, that the cemetery is still out there, forsaken and forgotten and that on moonlit nights the dead walk, looking for their homes and their kin."

Andi shuddered. "Gee, thanks for the information."

Henry laughed and opened a new bottle of wine. "Well you asked!" he exclaimed as he held the bottle to her.

She hesitated, but once again didn't want to be rude. Sipping, she savored the wine, fought back a twinge of guilt over giving in to weakness, then she shrugged and laughed too. "Guess I did, didn't I."

Henry took the bottle back and took a swig, "Just ignore me. As far as I know, I've never seen a ghost or heard one. Anyway, lots of strange stuff grow and live out here. It's a unique ecosystem. The key to becoming a local is to adapt, adjust and enjoy."

Andi nodded, thinking *good advice, hope I can do it*. "Does anyone know what happened to Janine? I mean it is wonderful that she left me her home and all, but she just … just… vanished."

He settled on the stool behind him and frowned. He sighed and his face took on a far away look. "Janine was a sweet girl, but an unhappy one. Grew up here. Drank, did drugs. She was a loner, must have been lonely and frustrated. I remember that the last time I saw her she was so morose. I guess she was done trying. The one thing about the pines and the marshes that run through them is if you want to disappear, well, it's easy to do and almost impossible to get found. I think she died, but maybe she just ran away back to the city. Either way, you got a sweet piece of property and with a little work, that place can be right as rain again. Just remember to buy all your supplies here!"

She sat and shared the bottle with him until it was empty and her head was spinning. She was amazed how it affected her after being sober for half a year. She smiled at the man in front of her hoping she looked enticing and hoping for a little action. It had been a long time since she'd had drunken sex.

He smiled back, "Well little lady, it's closing time and the wife's got dinner on the table. See you around sometime."

Andi felt like he'd slapped her. She was a failure at being a woman. She stood and walked out trying for dignity but staggered and settled for tipsy. Driving home slowly, exaggerating her movements, she was trying to make herself sober.

She was embarrassed. *God, hitting on an old, married man*, and it hit home once again that she certainly was lousy at attracting men. The wine fueling her thoughts she remembered how she'd never fit in anywhere she'd lived. She was forty-eight-years-old and forty-eight years-lonely. She'd thought about how she'd never known the love of a man, at least real love. Sex was easy, intimacy proved to be something impossible.

As Andi drove through the dusk, the deep shadows thrown by the trees darkened the road to night black and she began to cry. That was why Janine left her this place, Janine had recognized a kindred spirit, another soul lost in misery. "This was a place for the perpetually unhappy to dwell, a home for the wretched," she sobbed and looked out the open car window at bleak, lightless forest.

Drunk and depressed, she left her groceries in the car and stumbled to her bedroom and threw herself onto the bed. She was so sunk in self-pity she didn't have the strength to do anything more. The night was black when Andi woke and she felt inexplicably terrified. She opened her eyes wide and tried to see through the opaque wall of darkness, but couldn't see through it. She whimpered and knew that something had disturbed her sleep. She felt nauseous from both the wine and fear as she realized she hadn't locked up. She was still in her shorts, tee shirt and flip-flops.

And she was positive that there was someone in the house, someone in the bedroom with her. Andi could feel their presence and strained to hear them breathe, hear them make a sound. Sweat ran off her soaking her clothes and sheets. Her teeth started to chatter. Tears mixed with the perspiration. She couldn't move, she was paralyzed with fear. She was amazed that she could breathe, and more amazed that her heart kept beating.

Why didn't whoever it was make a move? Her vision had adjusted to the dark and she could swear that the deeper shadows in the corner of her bedroom began to swirl. She could physically feel it move closer to her.

Something snapped inside her and Andi could finally move a little. She opened her mouth to scream but no sound came out. She was petrified again. Waves of dizziness washed over her and she knew she was passing out, but just before she fainted, something velvety soft and gentle brushed her cheek and forehead like a parent to a child.

Then all was blackness.

***

She opened her eyes to a gray, dreary day, amazed she wasn't dead. Getting up, Andi ignored the wine headache. She stumbled to looked at herself in the dresser mirror and saw perfectly normal.

Rationalizing it'd been a dream. What else could it have been with the moving shadows and that caressing touch. she brewed a pot of coffee then realized that it was just too hot and humid to drink the stuff. She downed it anyway craving the caffeine kick, then poured a second cupful and walked into the sunroom. Wincing at the putrid smell, she stared in utter astonishment and began laughing despite herself. Of course she hadn't been raped in her bed last night because all the erect pink penises were now gray and flaccid, slumped to the floor.

She giggled feeling a rush of release from the tension of the night before and announced to the silent trees, "Men, they are only good for just so long and then…"

Andi drank her coffee and wondered what would grow next, but discovered she didn't really care anymore. "I'm going to tear down this room once this oppressive heat and humidity lifts. The

158

Barrens could just keep it shrooms to itself. I want that garden of fresh, colorful flowers and maybe some healthy vegetables."

She spent the morning reading a novel, forgetting about the mushrooms and almost forgetting about the bottle of wine on the kitchen counter. In early afternoon, the sky opened up and the rains came in short heavy showers. In between the squalls the heat would build up until it was hard to take a deep breath and a gray mist reached from the low clouds to the ground and then the rain would begin again, rushing down, pounding on her roof.

This lasted all day and well into the night. She tried to sleep, but the humidity was unbearable. Finally, she took the bottle of wine and a portable lamp out into the sunroom in hope of a breeze and tried to sleep on the dirty, plastic, sofa shoved to one side of the screened room. She was tired and uncomfortable, her hair was plastered to her face and the sweat beaded up and rolled off her continuously. Still she was grateful that the rusted screens were strong enough to keep the mosquitoes out. She could hear them buzzing, droning endlessly, trying to get through the mesh to feast on her. The fading battery operated light drew dozens of moths that settled on the screens and she ignored them knowing they were safely on the other side.

She lifted the now opened bottle to her lips and drank. She wasn't enjoying the wine, but she still drank it. Finishing off the entire bottle, she was so tipsy and miserable that she forgot to be scared of the boogie man she had imagined the night before. All she wanted to do was fall asleep and then in the

159

morning figure out how to get the air conditioner working again.

Eventually the buzzing bugs, the alcohol and the humidity lulled her into a comatose state and she fell into a fitful sleep. Thunder woke her and her small lamp had finally burned out. The sunroom was dimly lit by the lamp she'd left on in the living room.

Her eyes adjusted and she suddenly noticed the man. He stood in the middle of the sunroom, stood over the crack pulling his foot out of the impossibly small opening. She wanted to faint again, but couldn't. Her body was betraying her, not letting her escape from the thing about to happen. She was going to be aware of everything whether she wanted too or not. There'd be no escape.

Andi tried to close her eyes, hide from the vision, but she was like a statue, frozen. She stared as he turned toward her and she finally saw him clearly in the dim lamplight. He was gray and he was naked, but instead of being terrified, the vision of him calmed her. He was so beautiful, so perfect.

He gazed at Andi, caught her eye and smiled at her.

Amazed and not quite understanding what was happening, she smiled back.

The gray man moved to her and she surprised herself by moving as well.

Instead of backing away, Andi held out her arms to him knowing she was being totally irrational. He was a monster, not human, but she didn't care. She didn't know why, but she wanted him to come to her.

160

He sat beside her on the edge of the sofa, put his arms around her and hugged. She recognized the gentle velvety touch from the night before. It hadn't been a crazed dream, although she knew this ought to be one. He was smooth and soft yet solid enough to be a real man.

Holding her gently, kissing her face, kissing her throat, her breasts, he worked his way down Andi's body. A strong, moldy odor came off him, but she didn't mind, nor did she care about the oddly musty taste of him. With each kiss, she arched toward him, silently begging for more. She understood with each velvety caress that he was what had been missing from her world all her life. He was what she'd been looking for, waiting for.

He moved his lips back up to hers, and Andi kissed back with a hunger that was surprising. If he didn't take her now, she decided that she'd definitely die and go to hell. She had to have him completely.

Then he entered her and she moaned with pleasure. It was the only sound in the room as they moved together in unison, blending together.

And then it was over. He kissed her one last time. She knew a good-bye kiss when she felt one. He got up and touched her face, a gentle, loving caress, his skin mossy to the feel. His fingers lingered, for just a moment longer, then having never spoken a word, he walked back to the crack and slowly wilted. She started in horror and loss as he sank down into the dirt and disappeared. She watched him disappear and realized her heart was breaking for the first time ever.

After a second or two of hesitation, Andi suddenly jumped up.

"No!" she shrieked. "Don't leave me. I love you!" She dug at the concrete, breaking her nails, drawing blood, desperately trying to widen the pathway and get him back.

Eventually, she stopped. Weeping, she groaned, "Oh, help me, it's impossible, but I'm in love with a mushroom man." And despite her tears, she laughed bitterly at the absurdity of it. "It figures that something like this would happen to me."

She eventually fell asleep on the floor, her hand resting on the crack her fingers curled into the soil.

Waking to another gray, misty day, Andi watched the rain fall and noticed mushrooms sprouting up all over the back yard. The humidity was relentless and the heat seemed to steal all her strength. She never moved until she noticed that the crack was a little wider.

She dug at it listlessly, knowing it was hopeless.

Once again she was all alone. She cried most of the day, prone on the floor, mourning all the lost opportunities, the lost loves, the children never born. She wished more than ever that she could get up find another bottle and drink herself into oblivion. But it took too much energy to even think about it.

That night she lay there waiting, but he never came, nor the night after that.

Weak and hungry Andi woke on the third day to find gray, fuzzy patches on her arms, her legs, and other places where gray fuzzy patches just

162

didn't belong. She struggled to the shower and scrubbed at her skin, cleaning it off, then collapsed on her bed. Waking a few hours later, she saw more gray patches. This time after she scrubbed them off, her skin looked colorless, dull. Two more days, sleeping and showering until it hurt, didn't help at all. She studied herself in the mirror, she could see blue veins pulsing beneath her pale white skin as if it were growing thinner, losing layers.

"I've got to get to a doctor," she sighed, but went back to the damp, musty smelling bed instead to sleep some more.

A noise woke Andi and she pushed herself up to see Janine, naked and covered in gray fuzz, at the foot of the bed.

"They're spores," she said to Andi as she rubbed herself.

Andi tried to stand, but after five days with nothing to eat, she was too weak. "Oh how horrible!"

Janine smiled. "Not really, as they leave me and find a new home, they blossom into new life. They are my children, Andi, and I have thousands of children. My life finally has meaning. I heard you say this place is for the lost and the wretched, but you are wrong. I left it to you because this place is fulfillment. Don't let it slip away. Come with me. Come finally live your life. I knew you needed this as much as I did. Andi, you and me, we are kindred spirits. I knew that as soon as we met in Scranton."

Andi glanced down at her own arms and legs and saw that they were fully covered in what Janine had called spores. "This has got to be the ultimate fungal infection," she groaned. "I need help. I need the hospital. Help me."

Janine came over and half lifted Andi to her feet. "I'll help you. Come on."

Leaning on Janine, Andi struggled to walk.

Instead of going out the front door, they headed for the sunroom.

Andi, shook her head. "No, please, not this, help me!"

"I am." Janine said and pushed her into the room.

The concrete floor was gone, covered instead with soil and thousands of mushrooms. Andi fell forward into them, landing on her knees. She reached up to Janine imploringly with one hand and felt her other hand begin to sink into the loamy dirt.

She could feel herself being absorbed, her knees and legs slowly being swallowed by the ground cover. Too weak to struggle, she opened her mouth to beg again, just as a strong, perfect, gray hand reached out of the loam and took her outstretched fingers.

Andi knew it was his hand and suddenly wasn't afraid anymore. She clasped it back, their fingers intertwining, and she felt him pull her down, to live with him, to be loved under the Pine Barrens forever.

Stump Head (Andy Martin)

PITTSTOWN, MASSACHUSETTS 1878

At night in camp, Angus could look down and see the fires and the smoke from Pittstown. They made Pittstown seem so close, his bed, family and a good drink were just an easy walk down the road they'd been cutting into the hills.

Daylight told a different tale.

Angus mopped sweat from his brow and took a drink. He truly was just an hour or two's walk from his wife. How he missed her, her softness and scent making her seem an altogether different species from the sweating, stinking men he could hear cutting the road through the forest behind him.

He sat on fallen tree on the shore of a small lake, hidden from the valley by the hills and the forest. It was a splash of blue in the thick green of the forest, that same green that even now crowded the pitiful road they'd cut into it. And the road was the least of it. The clear cutting for Phipp's new mill hadn't even been begun. And the beaver dam which had created this lake and choked out the stream Phipps wanted to put his mill on? Still standing.

In the daylight, when Angus could measure his lack of progress in the impenetrable green all around him, home seemed very far away indeed.

Angus took another pull and stared at the lake. Behind him, his men cursed and chopped while the mules brayed and strained. He was close enough to the lake to see where the blue faded to a golden brown along the shore, given color by the plants at the bottom, looking from this angle like a lake of fine whisky. It was damned inviting.

He spat. Back to work.

Angus pushed off the stump, took one last look at the lake and turned-

A crack like thunder, so loud it could only *be* thunder except the sky was an empty blazing blue-white and then Angus heard the mules scream, followed by a second great crash and then another. Trees were falling, the only thing it could be, his men were screaming and he ran towards their screams as more crashes shook the forest-

Angus was hit in the chest, the air driven from his lungs. He fell, tangled, soaking wet and warm, to the forest floor. He sat up, gasping, and saw he was covered in blood.

Another great crack. More screams, men yelling, gibbering prayers, pleading for their mothers.

The thing that had knocked Angus down was lying in the moss and the pine needles, blood leaking from the ragged end. It was one of the mules' heads. Buttermilk, he thought.

Angus screamed and got to his feet, running towards the screams, picturing a block and tackle parting, a chain flying free, that could explain it-

He stopped at the head of the road.

The white birch trunks that ringed the clearing were splattered red like bloody bones and strewn with parts of men and mules.

"What-"

A footstep, heavy and sure behind him-

He turned and was flying, spinning, green moss and white trees and blue-white sky spinning around

him as below his tiny body crumpled at the feet of
the most terrible man Angus had ever seen-

***

"Lacey!"

Emma wrapped her arms around her and Lacey
pulled closer to her despite the summer heat. Emma
kissed her cheeks and then pushed back; her hands
tight around Lacey's forearms.

"I've missed you!" Emma said and now Lacey
pulled Emma close, squeezing her oldest friend and
breathing the sweet smell of her perfume and sweat,
the smell of what seemed like a thousand summer
nights spent walking the woods or sharing secrets in
Emma's bed.

"Oh how I missed you too!" Lacey replied.

"How is Boston?"

"Lovely but it doesn't compare to being here
and seeing your face again!" Lacey said and it was
true. She'd seen Paris and London and been living
in Boston, but nothing quite compared to the way
the summer light slanting through the parlor
windows lit Emma's face.

"Oh go on," Emma said but her eyes flashed
and Lacey knew she felt the same way.

"It's true, I've missed you so and-"

"Is that Lacey I hear?"

"It is!" Emma said as her smiling father entered
the parlor, smiling.

"Commodore!" Lacey said and Emma's father
held his arms out and Lacey folded into them. She
caught the familiar smell of the Commodore's after
shave and a hint of pipe smoke. A warm, inviting

smell, like Emma's, like that of the whole
Dunbarton house. It smelled like so much more of
home than Lacey's father's house did.

"And how is Boston? How is your father?" the
Commodore asked, holding Lacey's hands as if to
get a better look at her. "You've grown so, my
God," the Commodore said and grabbed Emma's
hand and pulled them shoulder to shoulder. "My
girls, together again. I'm so happy."

The girls hugged him and Lacey felt her own
heart breaking a little, the Commodore so unlike her
own father, the reception here so much warmer. The
Commodore released them.

"Boston is lovely and my studies are going
well-"

"She going to be a writer, father!" Emma
interjected.

"I'm sure you'll be a fine one. And Philip?"

"Good. He's been down at the mill all day and
I've only just arrived so I haven't seen him." Lacey
forced a smile as she said it and in truth a part of
her, a large part of her, was relieved that she hadn't
seen her father yet.

"Ah yes, there's been some trouble from what I
understand," the Commodore said.

"Yes, apparently a whole work gang ran off and
Father's been scrambling to replace them and
contact the constables."

The Commodore raised an eyebrow. "I didn't
realize it was so bad. Hard to imagine him having to
cast far and wide for more labor though, your father
and his mill have made Pittstown quite the
destination."

"Indeed," Lacey said, forcing a smile. Yes, her father, the Captain of Industry, the man who never visited, only wrote once a year, never offered an ounce of the compassion or the good feeling that the Commodore and Emma did. And his mill? A monstrosity that sat astride the river like a great brick spider, its smoke stacks looming over Pittstown.

The Pittstown Lacey had left was a green place, the forest crowding right to the edges of town. Now the whole valley was packed with tiny, rude houses and the forest had been cut back to the hillsides above the town.

Progress?

She thought not. The Commodore raised an eye brow as if he could read her thoughts, and quite possibly...agreed.

"Well, well, I shall leave you too it, but Lacey, you must come for dinner, say tomorrow?"

"Oh Father, she can't tomorrow, tomorrow we're going on a picnic!"

"A picnic?"

"I-" Lacey began,

"It was meant to be a surprise, but oh well. Some friends have a buckboard and there's been a new road cut into the forest and there's meant to be an absolutely lovely little lake at the end of it-"

"Emma, do you mean where the work crew absconded with Philip's wagon and equipment?" the Commodore asked, looking concerned.

"Oh Father, surely they must be miles from here. They're not lying about in the forests like brigands from some story. Besides, Jack and Harry will protect us," Emma said and took her father's arm, leading him back toward his study. She turned and winked at Lacey.

"Jack?" Lacey mouthed.

Emma gave her a smile that was fit for the devil and ushered her father back into his study where Lacey could still hear him talking about the runaway loggers…

***

Despite its size and placement on a point of land that jutted out into the river, Lacey's father's house, Morwen, was stifling in the summer heat. Lacey was in her room, looking out over the Androscoggin, her bags at the foot of her bed transferred from carriage to porter to maid without Lacey placing so much as a finger on them.

She'd drawn the line at letting the maids unpack them, though, she might have abdicated her independence for the duration of her brief stay at Morwen but there were limits. She opened her bags and then her dresser, the dark wood cool under her fingers. The wood was about the only thing cool and inviting in the house.

Not so much as a breeze stirred and though the windows were flung wide open the curtains hung limp. Below her even the river seemed sluggish with the heat, the water cloudy, sickly yellow foam gathering along the rocky shore and in the eddies. There was an undercurrent to the air as well, a faint stink like Boston harbor at low tide, nothing like the clean smell of the river she remembered from her youth.

Was this the progress her father had written of in his annual letter? A river stinking and slow, yellow foam where trout had once flashed brown and silver in the shallows? She filled the top drawer, paused once to see that her underthings were neat in the drawer and slid it out closed.

The walk back from the Dubartons' had done little to impress her with the 'progress' her father had wrought on Pittstown which was brown and dusty like she'd never known, the earth in the streets cracked and yawning in such a way that she could imagine the whole place turning into a morass with the help of the slightest rain. Only the hills across the new bridge were the same verdant green Lacey remembered from her youth.

It would be good to be among them tomorrow, if even for a day. She didn't intend to linger long in Pittstown, if anything, what had happened to the place made her want to flee to Boston as quickly as possible, despite how good it was to see Emma, but at least tomorrow seemed a pleasant diversion.

Of course, there was the issue of Jack to consider-

A knock brought her around. She placed her stockings in the next drawer down and slid it closed.

"Yes?"

"Your mother would like a word, ma'am..." came the maid's voice through the door. Lacey thought for a moment of the improbability of that statement. If her mother, her *real* mother, wanted a word it would have to be through one of those seances becoming so popular in Boston. The woman downstairs, only a decade Lacey's senior, was anything but her mother. Lacey looked herself

171

over in the mirror and decided she looked as presentable as the woman downstairs deserved and left her room.

The maid was already gone, flitted off like a nervous bird. Lacey hadn't gotten the poor thing's name yet and must do so, she thought. The heat of the hallway hit her like a wet towel and Lacey was sweating by the time she'd descended the single story to ground level and found her father's wife in the parlor.

"Mother," she said, choking the word out.

Dorcas Phipps was only a decade older than Lacey but she easily looked two or more older. In her youth her beauty had been what one could call severe, but now, she simply looked eroded, the skin pulled too tight around her sharp cheek bones and chin. The blue of her eyes had faded too, now they were grayer, like the surface of that slow, stinking river outside.

"Lacey, my dear," Dorcas said and nodded. "Your father asked me to bring you word he will not be home for supper."

"Trouble at the mill?" Lacey said.

Dorcas' upper lip, thin as a malnourished worm, jumped at that.

"No, nothing like that. Just the demands of business," Dorcas said.

Lacey nodded. "Well, perhaps I should go down there and see if I can offer assistance-"

Dorcas started at that. "Oh no, surely there's no need, I have Mary Ellen laying up supper as we speak-"

Lacey took a step forward and Dorcas took a step further back into the corner of the parlor. Up close the winnowing effect was even more plain. She looked eroded alright and Lacey had no doubt of the name of the storm that had done the damage.

"Mother," Lacey said, and took another step forward. "It has been 18 months since last I I saw my father and if he will not deign to see me at home, I shall seek him out at the Mill."

Lacey turned and made for the door, her father's wife calling after her.

***

Lacey had a moment of doubt as she walked to the edge of Pittstown in the late afternoon heat, if her father's house with its soaring ceilings and large open windows had been almost unbearable, how hot would his accursed brick monstrosity of a mill be? Surely it would be unbearable, but luckily for Lacey, she found her father in the Mill's courtyard.

The Phipps Paper Mill was separated from the road by a brick wall of roughly man-height) there was plenty of stone in Pittstown, it was New England after all, but only the most modern materials for Elihu Phipps. The Mill towered above the walls, radiating heat as it were a kiln instead of a paper mill.

It was nearing quitting time, it had to be, but she could hear the mill's machinery roaring inside and something else too, something that sounded an awful lot like shouting. She rounded the Mill's gates and found a chaotic scene.

A dozen or so women in threadbare dresses and sack cloth were gathered in the mill's courtyard, while at least half and again as many dirty children huddled around their legs like small birds.

Her father and a knot of large men, including Constable Black, were at the top of the Mill's steps facing the crowd. Behind them the mill doors were thrown wide and Lacey could see into the pits, see the massive saw blades spinning as men shouted and strained and maneuvered a huge tree into position.

"Where's my husband?" a woman at the head of the crowd screamed. "You sent your man to rifle through our house, to upset my bairns, but not to help, not to find him, no! You send them to look for any little bit and bob he might have squirreled away! Where's my husband, Mr. Phipps?"

Lacey's father seemed to have eroded like his wife. He was sweating, his hair plastered to his forehead, his mustache doing nothing to hide the gauntness of his face. His sleeves were rolled up as if he himself had been working the Mill's machinery.

"I sent the Constable round to answer that very question madam. Count yourself lucky it wasn't me and my men doing the asking!" he roared. "Your husband and his gang of layabouts have cost me quite a lot, and before you come to my door shouting accusations, perhaps you should remember who holds the deed to your house and help yourself and give me his whereabouts!"

Lacey felt sick to her stomach. Her father hadn't noticed her yet, he simply continued reading the woman the riot act, somehow no color rising to his cheeks, the only consideration to the heat and his fury the sweat that shone on his skin.

174

"Angus would never leave us! Steal a wagon and run away from me and the bairns? Never, not in a thousand years!" she screamed and took a step forward.

Constable Black looked uneasy as she advanced and looked at her father as if unsure of what to do. The grossly fat law man was sweating too, but it looked more as if he was sweating at the prospect of having to deal with this distraught woman than from the heat.

"Does this woman speak for all you then?" Lacey's father said, pushing passed the Constable, his men following, huge men, barrel chested with forearms as big around as Lacey's thigh. "You there, Mrs. O'Brian, does this harridan represent you and your family? And you, Mrs. Cleaves? What about you?"

Her father was a horror, a cold man whose only emotion was anger, but somehow he'd been gifted with the ability to remember names and faces better than anyone Lacey had ever known. The mill must have employed hundreds by now but he knew every one of these women by name.

"Does she?" he roared.

The women in the crowd backed away from the woman, pulling their children with them. The fury had gone out of the woman and she was looking around her, alone despite the cluster of children at her feet.

Across the newly formed circle of bare, cracked earth that had formed around her, the women were shaking their heads.

"Right. Then I expect you will assist the Constable here with any inquiries about your husbands. As for you and your litter, Mrs. Stuart, you will quit all Mill property, meaning your house, by sundown." Lacey's father looked up at the sun where it rode low over the river, the light already going orange. "Which is quite soon. So get moving or I'll have my men assist you."

"No, you can't! Where will we go, it's miles-"

"None of my concern. Constable Black, please, get this wretch and her brood off my property," he said and as he turned his eyes caught Lacey's and held them for a moment. He shrugged.

Lacey imagined a knife in her hand, imagined stabbing the bastard right there on the steps, imagined watching his blood pour out in front of these destitute women. Who cared if their husbands had made off with a wagon and some tools? How much value could there possibly be in those things? Lacey watched her father walk into the mill followed by his workers, the Constable shuffling toward them like screaming Stuart woman, the rest of the women and their children passed Lacey and into the street.

All Lacey could see was the mill's open door and then her father appeared in a window thirty feet to the right of it. He came to the window and caught her eyes. He didn't motion, made no effort to invite her forward or entreat her to come in, he simply looked at her, the open doors the only invitation Lacey would get.

Lacey held his gaze for another moment and then spat in the dust.

She turned as quick as she could but still, across the courtyard and through the mill window, she caught his smirk.

Bastard.

***

The sun had nearly set when Lacey got within sight of Morwen. The huge house stood hot and still in the ugly glow of sunset. Despite herself, Lacey could feel tears tracking through the dust in her cheeks.

Her father was awful.

Morwen was awful.

Pittstown, stripped of all its green, now yellow and brown in the fading rust of sunset, was awful.

She'd be damned if she'd spend another minute in that house while she was here, so she turned and went back towards Pittstown, making the turn at the Dunbarton's lane. Here the landscape changed as if in anticipation of the home she'd find at the end of the lane. The Commodore's fields were green with waist high corn in the field and great gnarled oaks dotted and shaded the lawn. Night came on as she reached the front walk and here it was the Pittstown of old; crickets sang and a breeze stirred the night air.

She paused under an oak and dabbed at her face, hoping to clear the dust and the tracks of her tears. The Dunbarton house was lit by lamps and candles and she could see the Commodore in his study, a pipe smoking on the end table neck to him, the big man's man chin folded into his chest. A candle burnt in Emma's window.

Just like when they were children, Lacey bent and found a pebble. She took aim and hit the window sill with a gentle *pock*. She knelt again, the

177

breeze building around, the crickets singing louder, the awful scene at the Mill, the coldness of her father's fury seeming miles away and years ago-

She threw and a giggling Emma ducked back into the window.

She reappeared. "You nearly killed me!" she shout-whispered down. Emma looked down at her, really seeing her and Lacey realized maybe she hadn't cleaned herself up as well as she'd hoped. "Your father?"

Lacey nodded, the tears coming again, suddenly feeling very small, feeling like all this had happened dozens of times before because it had-

"I'm coming," Emma said and disappeared from the window and when Emma eased the front door open and stood there, arms open, Lacey went to her and remembered that, despite it all, she did have a home in Pittstown.

***

Black leaned on the 'Pittstown, Massachusetts' sign and pulled a flask from his pocket. The Stuart woman and her litter had no lantern but he could still see them easily enough by moonlight as they shuffled out of town. He could hear them too, the woman had long since gone from screaming and pleading with him to a kind of quiet steely resolve which was somehow more annoying, but as they faded into the dark, Black could hear her trying to console the children as they shuffled along, their meager belongings on their backs.

Pathetic, Black thought and took another pull. But that's what you got, wife of a dirty Scots thief.

And probable murderer, Black thought and started making his way back towards town, the heat and his weight making progress slow.

When Phipps had reported his men missing, Black had borrowed a horse and ridden up the narrow little road the men had cut into the hills. The wagon was gone, and there was no trace of the men and their belongings, but there had been much blood. The trees lining the road they'd been cutting had been fairly soaked in the stuff, their trunks splattered a deep maroon. There'd been a thunderstorm the other night so Black thought it might have washed away by now, but at the time the clearing at the head of the road looked like an abattoir.

He'd told Mr. Phipps about it, told him he was sure the Scot had gone mad and killed the men but that he hadn't found their bodies. Of course, Black hadn't gone looking for them either and Mr. Phipps was sharp enough to know that, but between the blood and the funny trackways through the forest, the trees not so much cut as bent and still living, Black had thought it best to get out of there and get back to town.

Black stopped.

"Who are you then?" he shouted, trying to stuff his flask in his pocket but it snagged, nearly tipping onto the road,. He scrabbled for it, caught it and got it situated. Then he went to the stone wall separating the road from the steep river bank.

God, the river stinks tonight, he thought. In the moonlight, he could see rafts of yellow foam clinging to the shore.

Black could also see a man standing waist deep in the river. He was a very tall man and was wearing some sort of huge hat.

"You there!" Black shouted and leaned forward on the wall. He realized he might be in danger of slurring his words, or at best he was out of breath. "You! What are you doing? There's no fishing in that river!" The man turned towards him. Black got a brief glimpse before a cloud passed over the moon. He saw it was more of a hood than a hat the man was wearing. In the river and in disguise?

Black leaned farther out over the wall.

"You, come up there! Come up here now! I'm Constable Black and I demand to know what you're doing in that river!"

The clouds parted again. Black saw the man had something in his hand, then the section of wall collapsed. Black's weight carried him forward and he was rolling down the river bank, dirt filling his mouth and stones biting and beating him. The impossible sight of a tree root flexing and pulling down the wall burned in his head as he rolled-

Black hit the stony shore and the air was driven from his lungs. The stink of the river filled his nose and he threw up where he lay, half in the river and half on shore.

"You!" was all he managed as he pushed himself to his knees-

He heard a long splash, realizing a second too late that it was really a long series of splashed because the man in the hood was surging toward him and Black got his hands up then he was toppling sideways, trying to stop himself, no pain, just an enormous pressure and a strange cold

180

numbness at the end of his arms, like plunging them into ice water, but he couldn't stop himself and face planted on the bank. He couldn't push himself up or turn over because he couldn't seem to make contact with the ground. He screamed and rolled onto his back and it was raining, a hot sticky rain and when he forced his eyes open he screamed because both his arms were gone just below the elbow and the hooded man was above him and as the axe flashed down the last thing Black heard was the axe biting into the stone beneath his head, the sound's signal jumping across the gap of neurons newly parted. The hooded man dropped his axe, caught hold of Black's arm stumps and pulled him apart like a wish bone and flung the halves into the river.

***

It wasn't as if the ascent into the green hills overlooking Pittstown completely erased the pain of Lacey seeing her father cast a probable widow and her children onto the road but it did somehow make it more... *distant*. As they climbed the new and narrow road, like ascending a staircase into the forest, the ugliness at the mill, the iciness of her step mother's reception, all of it seemed, well, *below* her, like all that tension and trouble was bound in brown and yellow Pittstown and she was safe again in the green and gold woods where she'd whiled away so much of her youth.

Well, not exactly the same. These woods were wilder somehow, the green and gold of the leaves so bright they almost hurt her eyes, the singing of the

181

birds and the crash of squirrels in the undergrowth louder than she remembered. The felled timbers along the road were already being reclaimed by the forest, green moss coating the trunks and vines lacing among them.

"I imagine if your father doesn't get another crew up here soon this road will have to be recut by the winter, ow!," Harry said over his shoulder and Lacey stifled a laugh as she saw Emma's small elbow catch him under his ribs.

Emma pivoted in her seat in the front of the buckboard, her eyes flashing in the forest light. "There will be no talk of work, or lumber, or fathers today, Harry. We're on a picnic!"

Harry mumbled an apology over his shoulder and snapped the reigns. They sped up just slightly, the going was still rough and uphill, but the tree trunks flicked by faster now. Lacey leaned back in her seat and watched the sky through the tree tops, it was a deep perfect blue, a cool blue, the type that spoke of summer warmth without yesterday's stifling heat.

"It's beautiful day for it, isn't it?" Jack asked, shifting in his seat next to her.

Jack. He was handsome, built more like one of the lumber men than the aspiring account he was but there was also something so unaccountably dull about him as well. And not just in his personality, there was something dull about his good looks too, as if his attractiveness was born out of something like a math equation, his broad chest and white teeth and strong jaw all adding up on paper at least, to *handsome,* but in the flesh, he was somehow lacking.

182

They'd known each other since childhood and there'd been a few brief kisses and fumblings in the woods after dances during their youth but Lacey had largely forgotten Jack while she'd been in Boston and she almost resented Emma bringing him out here today, as if Emma in her own way was trying to rope her back into a life in Pittstown.

Lacey thought again about the scene at the mill and vowed that despite her love for Emma and the Commodore she could never come back here again. She absorbed the warmth of the sun and the relief all hit her at once and she beamed.

Jack leaned forward and laid a massive hand on her forearm.

The poor dim boy, Lacey thought.

"Sorry, it is lovely but I was a million miles away," Lacey said. Jack looked stung but what could she do?

"Oh look!" Emma squealed and bounced in her seat, moving to the side so Lacey and Jack could see and there, as promised, was a splash of blue through the tree trunks.

Lacey couldn't deny the beauty in the little lake, not much more than a beaver pond really, but beautiful all the same-

"It is lovely!" Lacey agreed and for no reason at all, beyond the sun and the warmth and the beauty of it all she reached over and squeezed Jack's forearm.

Ahead, the road ended, not in a cul de sac as was to be expected but it simply faded into the trees, a large beech tree down at the head of the road and lying across it an angle. Beyond it the trees rose skyward and mighty, except for a single black green

183

trunk half again as tall as a man. Despite the beauty of the gallery forest and the lake shining beyond, there was something that chilled Lacey about the way road ended-

"Are you all right?" Jack asked.

Emma turned in her seat. "Lacey?"

"I'm fine, it's lovely, a goose must have walked over my grave. Really, I'm fine."

The horses were hauled up on the reins and the sounds of the forest rushed in to overwhelm their snorting and nicking as they stopped just short of where the road melted into the wood.

Harry dismounted and hitched the horses to a branch before returning to help Emma down, Jack, emboldened by Lacey's touch, vaulted over the side of the buckboard and came around to help her down.

"Thank you," she said and shook free of his arm as gently as she could once her feet were on the forest floor. Her shoes sunk into the moss and the leaf litter, the forest seeking to reclaim this road, to heal the wound from the ground up-

There was something slightly horrifying about that image, a riot of green vines and creeping moss and roots pulling the forest together like sutures-

"Lacey, are you alright?" Emma asked.

Lacey fanned herself. "Quite. I think in my time in Boston I've simply forgotten about how alive, how *green* the forest can be."

"Yes, it's positively primal, isn't it?" Jack said, taking a step closer to them, his presence crowding Lacey to an uncomfortable degree-

"That's almost the way those Irish ran off, makes a kind of sense, doesn't it?" Harry said.

"They were Scots and what did I say, Harry?" Emma said, dropping Lacey's hand and stepping towards her.

Harry swooped in, caught her around the waist and Emma shrieked. "Put me down!"

"Only once we reach my forest lair!" Harry shouted and Emma shriek laughed as Harry stepped over the felled log and bore her off toward the lake.

"Lacey, help!" Emma shouted, laughing, half-heartedly kicking at Harry-

Lacey took a step forward and Jack caught her arm, she turned on him, Harry and Emma disappearing into the shifting green shadows of the forest-

"What?"

"Forgive me, I may have arranged that with Harry."

Lacey took a step toward him and gathered herself up.

"Why?"

Jack looked hurt, whatever he planned unraveled all over his broad, blandly attractive and frankly stupid face-

"I, I, it had just been so long, Lacey, and I wanted to talk to you alone-"

"Well, forgive me for being brusque, Jack, but I don't see that we have much to discuss," Lacey said and turned away, scanning the green forest, something absent there that was disturbing her now, making her wish she and Emma had never come. She tried chalking it up to guilt, like the daughter of a monster like her father didn't deserve an afternoon folly after he'd turned a poor widow out, but it was more than guilt, it was a palpable sense that something was suddenly very wrong and quite possibly dangerous.

"Lacey!"

Lacey tore off into the forest, catching a glimpse of Emma's white dress up ahead, her laughing screams confirming her presence before she disappeared into the green.

"Lacey!" Jack whined and Lacey was glad she couldn't see that handsome face looking so pathetic as she chased her friend to the lake-

***

Harry put Emma down roughly, her back to a tree, the blue lake with the golden shallows just a few feet away. A flight of wood ducks careened off the lake, whistling and bouncing away from them across its surface.

"Brute!" Emma said, sprang forward to throw her arms around Harry's neck and pulled him close for a kiss. "I'll show you who's the savage," she said and pressed herself against him-

The forest had gone silent save for the whistling of the agitated wood ducks as they skittered further from shore-

***

The silence of the forest pressed in on Lacey like the humidity of Pittsfield except it was somehow worse. Pittsfield's oppression had felt like something familiar, but this felt like something altogether different, more animal, almost predatory.

And there was something else. Something frankly impossible. Back where the road was consumed by the wood, she was sure something was missing.

At least Jack had gone silent behind her, the lunk no doubt pouting by the buckboard.

***

Harry pulled back, unbuttoning his trousers and stepping out of them. Emma sat on a tree stump a few feet away, unbuttoning her under skirts.

"How do you think Lacey and Jack are getting on?" Harry said.

Emma screwed up her face as somewhere above them clouds moved over the tree tops and threw the silent forest into shadow. "Grand, I'm sure. He is awfully handsome and she quite fancied him when she was young. But I fear Jack will get the short end of it because for Lacey I don't think he'd be more than but an afternoon's diversion - what?"

The shadow fell across Harry and Emma heard something like the scrape of tree branches in the wind and Harry screamed. Emma dove forward and Harry's scream cut off and as she was scrambling to her hands and knees, making sure to run away from the lake, toward the path, toward Lacey, toward the road, she saw the axe complete its sideways arc and Harry's head was gone above his nose, blood geysering from the pink meat above his slack mouth-

***

"Lacey!" Emma screamed from somewhere up ahead, shattering the silence of the green wood and then Lacey was sprinting through the wood, hearing her dearest friend screaming, panting, crashing towards her-

"RUN, LACEY!" Emma screamed again-

"No," Lacey said or thought, she didn't know which and then screamed, "I'm coming, Emma!" and charged forward-

It wasn't a clearing, it wasn't as wide as that, it wasn't much more than a game trail that slanted towards the lake and Lacey saw Emma, her legs bare, her white dress billowing behind her and Lacey's eyes sought Emma's and they met, the terror in Emma's eyes filling hers even as Lacey saw movement behind Emma, like a great, mossy black tree falling and then a brilliant flash of polished steel and an explosion of red as the axe fell and split Emma from the crown of her head to her crotch.

"EMMA!"

A huge man, dressed in some shaggy, mossy, green-black pea coat pulled his axe free of the forest floor, the moss all around it subsumed in the great red tide spilling from Emma's bifurcated halves and Lacey's eyes were searching for the man monster's eyes, to scream, to gouge, to tear and found only an impossible mask, a massive, eyeless, tree stump where his head should be, severed roots curling down his chest like inverted antlers-

"EMMA!" Lacey howled like a threat, a *vow* and then turned on her heels and bolted for the buckboard-

***

"Jack, Jack, RUN!" Lacey screamed as the end of the road resolved itself and there was no longer silence, instead there was a cacophony of sounds, the huge, terrible man crashing through the forest behind her, the horses screaming and neighing ahead of her and somewhere in between a sound like rain falling on the leaves. She caught sight of the horses suddenly bathed in red rain and the heat of it, the stink, hauled her up and she jumped back and followed the awful rain to its source and there were pieces of Jack, his limbs broken and draped over tree branches, his guts dangling above her, a tree branch threaded up and out of his square jaw-

Lacey felt the axe coming and the trance broke and she dove to the side as it connected with the tree above her.

Lacey rolled and saw the terrible man recoil as if he'd been struck himself, his long, lanky body in his thread bare, moss encrusted pea coat and trousers shuddering, his black gloved hands flying free of the axe handle as he staggered back, no sound coming from beneath that hideous, eye-less stump mask, just a rattle like branches in a winter wind and then Lacey was on her feet, sliding in Jack's gore but she planted her feet as she saw the towering man recovering, shaking his stump mask, steadying himself-

Lacey planted a foot against the trunk and pried the axe free just as the terrible man was staggering towards her, long fingers outstretched and Lacey

189

buried the axe in his chest and he toppled backward without a sound.

"DIE!"

Lacey pulled the axe free, was splattered in some sticky-sweet, amber substance and brought the axe down over her head, once, twice, thrice and there was a crack and she was splattered again in that sweet tasing ichor and the stump mask rolled free-

There was no blood.

There was no torn flesh.

Above the ragged collar of the threadbare peacoat were only bark and vines, sap spilling from the wounds her ax had made-

Her eyes found the stump mask as it righted itself on its great gnarled roots. The roots groped through the leaf litter like an octopuses' tentacles, grabbing for the man shaped 'corpse' on the forest floor but sending new roots out, writhing searching, winding around trunks of trees and fallen logs-

Lacey pulled the axe from the corpse at her feet as the first of the roots caught hold and ran for the horses-

***

Elihu Phipps' stood in his mill, sweating and contemplating the end of his empire.

The mill had high ceilings and the second flood was dominated by huge windows, the expense of which had nearly scuttled the whole thing but would, he'd been assured, allow the mill to operate even longer in the day. Men wrestled a log onto the

190

saws and began cutting it into long planks, the better to be pulped into paper.

Even those longer hours weren't enough though, not with the mill and the portion of Pittstown that he'd owned mortgaged to the hilt. No, there weren't enough hours in the day and his experiments in men pulping by gas light had resulted in a man losing both his arms above the elbow. So, Phipps stood in the mill himself, sweating, shouting orders and trying keep his mind off the fact that Morwen and the mill and all the rest would very likely soon be gone.

It was why he'd been so angered by the disappearance of those twelve men; first, he had orders to fill and couldn't spare them, but more importantly, if they'd finished the road to the lake in the hills and undammed it, the flow from the hills would have enabled him to build the second mill and increase production. Despite the horror of the initial expense, it might be enough to save him and Pittstown.

"Sir!"

Phipps turned.

It was Barlow, a big man, one of the few men truly loyal workers Phipps had.

"What?" Phipps hollered, blocking his ears against the screaming of the saw.

"Sir, come, please!" Barlow shouted, as above them, men on the second floor, men with a better look out the windows were shouting for their fellows and all around him, men were shouting and rushing, but worse, the saws were falling silent-

There was no asking why for Phipps.

"Damn your eyes, all of you, back to work! Back to work!" Phipps screamed and lunged across the mill floor, heading for the doors. "Back to work! Back to work!" he screeched, mortified by the crack in his voice but unable to contain his fury as what few men he had left ignored him and raced back and forth on the floor, screaming, grabbing each other, seeming unsure as to whether they should flee or lock the doors-

"The door! Bar the door!" a man screamed and men were bolting past Phipps, knocking him aside, nearly knocking down as he slapped and clawed at them, screaming at them to get back to work and then Barlow was there, throwing men aside, grabbing for Phipps-

"Here sir, come please, please God what is it?" Barlow stammered and pulled Phipps through the door into the blinding midday heat. The door crashed shut behind them and Barlow screamed, looked at the road and then the door and then the road again and then at Phipps and moaned "sir... my children!" and Barlow was running towards Pittstown-

A red nightmare was coming down the road into the hills above Pittstown and as that red nightmare came closer, Phipps realized the blood covered woman on the horse was his daughter Lacey.

But what followed her was impossible and so much worse-

***

192

Lacey couldn't comprehend the thing that was chasing her, but she knew on some level where she wanted to lead it.

The Pittstown Road leveled out and her father's mill was ahead on her left. She lashed at the horse beneath her, trying to turn it, felt its terror, its need to keep racing for the horizon but then it started to heel to the left as if it too understood what Lacey wanted.

She looked behind her to make sure it hadn't changed its course and still it surged on, just thirty yards behind her, so green and black it almost burned against the brown dust of Pittstown-

The stump headed thing had assembled a new body somehow, the stump sitting atop an enormous, mossy, worm-like body made from several great logs twisted together and pulled forward on dozens of branch legs, like the world's largest, most terrible caterpillar. Still, it had no eyes, just that broad, vaguely octopus shaped stump, the front pair of asymmetrical roots curving down like the mandibles of an enormous insect.

Lacey pulled hard on the horse's mane and the horse responded and curved into the mill gates. Ahead of her Lacey could see people fleeing the grounds and a second later there was a great explosion and bricks were flying through the air ahead of her, smashing in the mill's windows, screams pouring out even as Lacey saw her father looking small and terrified but rooted to the spot just outside the shaking, locked doors and Lacey pulled the horse hard to the right, spinning it in a circle, the word tilting crazy, sure the horse would break a leg or throw her and as the world spun she saw her father suddenly run away from his mill as the great tree-worm collided with it like a locomotive and the whole left side of the mill collapsed around in a deluge of brick and timber and dust-

The explosion was too much and the horse bucked and screamed and Lacey was thrown even as she saw the collapse that had begun on the mill's left side spread, the mill leaning towards it great wound first and then falling into it and disappearing in a red cloud as Lacey hit the ground and knew nothing more.

***

"Lacey!"

Lacey came to and vomited. Her whole body hurt and her mouth tasted of brick dust and blood.

Her father loomed over her, something like concern on his sharp features. Lacey blinked hard, saw that he too was caked in brick dusk. There was blood in his hair.

She allowed her father to pull her into a sitting position and the world spun around and Lacey *remembered*. All of it. The carnage in the woods, the thing that looked like a man but was not and had become a worm and chased her here. The collapse of the mill which was even now forcing itself into her consciousness as the cries of dying men reached her ears.

But most of all, what she thought of, who she thought of, was Emma.

"Bastard!" she screamed and slapped at her father's hands.

"Lacey, please, you must help me!" She shoved him and got to her feet, suddenly aware of just how much blood was in his hair and realized he was hurt quite badly.

"You did this! Your, your mill, it brought that, that thing," she said and as she staggered away, she pointed toward the mill-

"Oh no."

The pile of smoking rubble to the left side of the mill was shifting.

Village men, women, wives, widows on the great smoking pile of bricks suddenly stopped digging, looked unsure of themselves, the canniest among them starting to run while behind it the Androscoggin flowed sluggish and yellow in the nightmare late afternoon heat-

"Lacey!" her father screamed and it was then that Lacey realized he must have crawled to her because his left leg was broken bad enough for bone to show. Behind him the pile shifted again and there was no indecision, the would-be rescuers were fleeing, running past the Phipps father and daughter as an avalanche of brick and timber flowed down the pile and Lacey screamed as she saw that eyeless stump appear first, like an otter's head in a river of brick and then the body followed, huge, towering, limbs cobbled together from split planks and logs yet to be split, iron tie downs and braces running through it and bricks sticking to the newly shorn timbers of the great thing as it took one, then another, faltering but massive steps out of the pile.

And in one of its hands, was a log with a man-sized circular saw blade fitted on the end.

It made no sound except for the great rumble of its movement, timber, iron, and brick all grinding against each other to announce its progress.

Lacey began to run and the great thing swung its improvised axe wide like a scythe through the fleeing rescues, shearing through them, blood and arms and heads flying into the air as the citizens of Pittsfield fell bleeding and in pieces all over the road in front of the mill.

Still the thing came on, clearing the rubble pile and crossing the distance between the mill and her father in two great steps.

"Lacey!" her father keened as the great tree man stopped and looked down at him.

"Lacey!" her father screamed again as the tree man slowly twisted the saw blade from its log hilt-

"Please, please no!" her father cried, his hand folded in prayer above him, the tree man's stump head tilted down at him. The tree man worked the blade free and started walking again, dropping it on her father in passing like a man tossing a coin to a beggar. His scream cut off with a squelch as the pulverized goo of Pittsfield's richest citizen spurted from under the saw blade.

Lacey couldn't out run the thing so she stopped and tried to stand tall in the heat and the screams and the stink of blood and brick and shit. The thing looked down at her, eyeless, but she could feel the stump with the pronged roots regarding her.

"His house is just there," she said and pointed up the road to where Morwen stood proud over the Androscoggin.

The shifting man shaped pile of timber and brick and iron regarded her for another moment.

She wanted to rage at it, to attack its legs, but what would that do beside end her own life? Emma was gone. Her father was gone. What was there to fight for in this place her father had destroyed?

The stump turned away from her toward Morwen, and the thing set off, its gait ever more unsure with each step, great hunks of timber and iron falling to the ground in a rain of bricks. Lacey watched as it stepped over the garden walls at Morwen, one of its great arms breaking free and landing in the front yard. She truly hoped the servants weren't home.

Somehow, over the screams of the dying all around her, Lacey heard Drocas' shrill cry scream as the great thing raised its remaining arm and lunged forward and then its great weight was on Morwen, driving down and through the house in a cloud of plaster and white dust, and the great tree man took her father's house off the bluff and collapsed with it into the river.

Meet the authors

Damir Salkovic is the author of the sci-fi thriller "Kill Zone", the occult mystery "Always Beside You", and short stories featured in multiple horror and speculative fiction magazines and anthologies, including the Lovecraft eZine, Thirteen O'Clock Press, Strange Aeon, and Scare Street's "Night Terrors" series. An auditor by trade and traveler by heart, he does his best writing on cruise ships, thirty-plus thousand feet in the air, and in the terminals of far-flung airports. He lives in Virginia with his wife. When not writing fiction, he reviews horror movies, discusses books, and shares his unsolicited opinions on just about everything on his blog, Darker Realities.

Sandra Stephens is a writer living in the Pacific Northwest with her husband and chocolate Labrador, Jake. She has published several shorts in the horror genre, and while she doesn't always write horror, she likes to imagine the most horrific turn of events in any circumstance, making her an excellent dinner party conversationalist.

Thomas   M.   Malafarina (www.ThomasMMalafarina.com) has published seven horror novels, as well as seven collections of horror short stories. He has also published a book of often strange single panel cartoons called Yes I Smelled It Too, as well as a Microsoft based technical manual called Link-Tuit. He has written and published more than 200 short stories. All of his horror books have been published through Hellbender Books an imprint of Sunbury Press. (www.Sunburypress.com).

Carl Hughes is a writer and journalist who has worked for the national and provincial press in the UK and has had his articles published worldwide, from the UK to Australia, India to the US. His fiction has appeared in many anthologies and magazines and he has won numerous writing competitions. He specialises in writing about the offbeat and bizarre, with a special love of horror and *Twilight Zone*-type stories. He is married and lives in Norfolk with wife Linda.

Diane Arrelle has more than 350 short stories published and two short story collections: Just A Drop In The Cup and Seasons On The Dark Side. She, her sane husband and insane cat live on the edge of the New Jersey (USA) Pine Barrens (home of the Jersey Devil).
www.arrellewrites.com FaceBook: Diane Arrelle

Andy Martin is an archaeologist, musician, and writer living in South Philadelphia with his partner and their cat. An avid outdoorsman, his writing takes as much inspiration from his time spent in the woods and on the water as it does classic horror novels and movies. His writing has appeared in Midnight Tales, Sirens Call, the Horror Tree, and he was DandT Publishing's Emerge Author in December 2022.